THE LEGEND OF SLEEPY HOLLOW

by Washington Irving

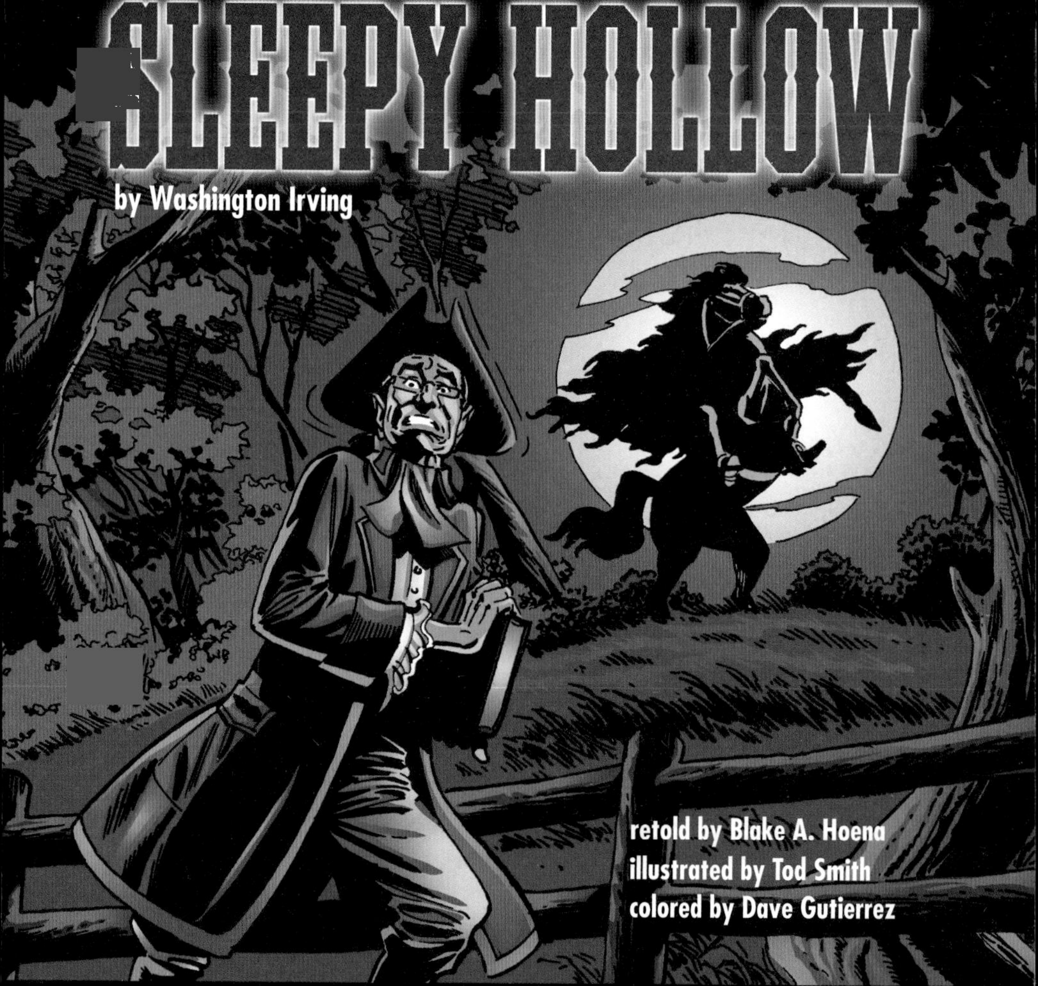

retold by Blake A. Hoena
illustrated by Tod Smith
colored by Dave Gutierrez

LIBRARIAN REVIEWER
Katharine Kan
Graphic novel reviewer and Library Consultant, Panama City, FL
MLS in Library and Information Studies, University of Hawaii at Manoa, HI

READING CONSULTANT
Elizabeth Stedem
Educator/Consultant, Colorado Springs, CO
MA in Elementary Education, University of Denver, CO

STONE ARCH BOOKS
MINNEAPOLIS SAN DIEGO

Graphic Revolve is published by Stone Arch Books,
A Capstone Imprint
151 Good Counsel Drive, P.O. Box 669,
Mankato, Minnesota 56002.
www.capstonepub.com

Library of Congress Cataloging-in-Publication Data
Hoena, B. A.
    The Legend of Sleepy Hollow / Washington Irving (retold by Blake A. Hoena);
illustrated by Tod Smith.
        p. cm. — (Graphic Revolve)
    ISBN 978-1-4342-0446-2 (library binding)
    ISBN 978-1-4342-0496-7 (paperback)
    1. Graphic novels. I. Smith, Tod. II. Irving, Washington, 1783–1859. Legend of
Sleepy Hollow. III. Title.
PN6727.H57L44 2008
741.5'973—dc22   2007030807

Summary: A headless horseman haunts Sleepy Hollow! At least that's the legend in the
tiny village of Tarry Town. But scary stories won't stop the town's new schoolmaster,
Ichabod Crane, from crossing through the Hollow, especially when the beautiful Katrina
lives on the other side. Will Ichabod win over his beloved or discover that the legend of
Sleepy Hollow is actually true?

Art Director: Heather Kindseth
Graphic Designer: Brann Garvey

Printed in the United States of America in Stevens Point, Wisconsin.
102012
006968R

TABLE OF CONTENTS

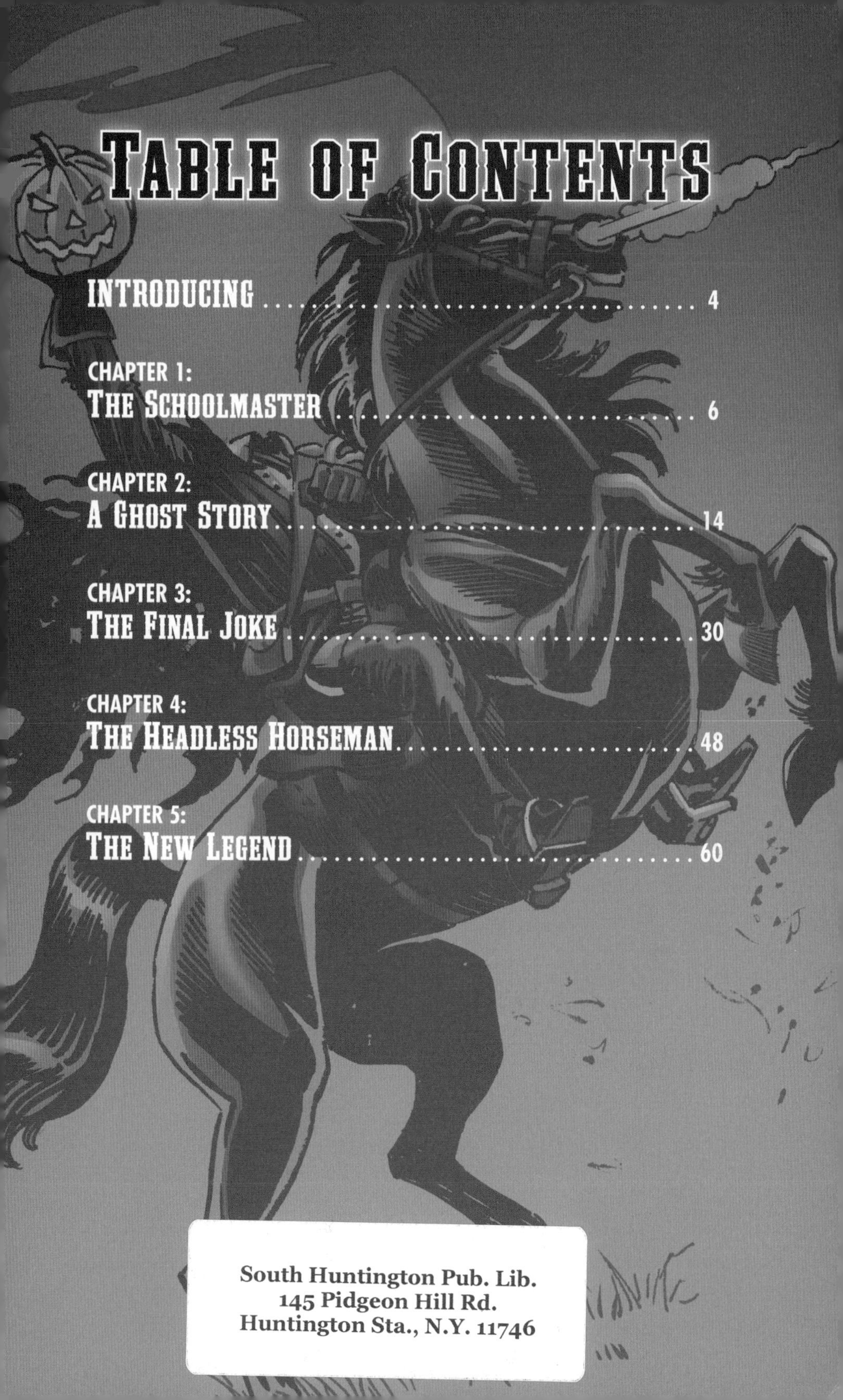

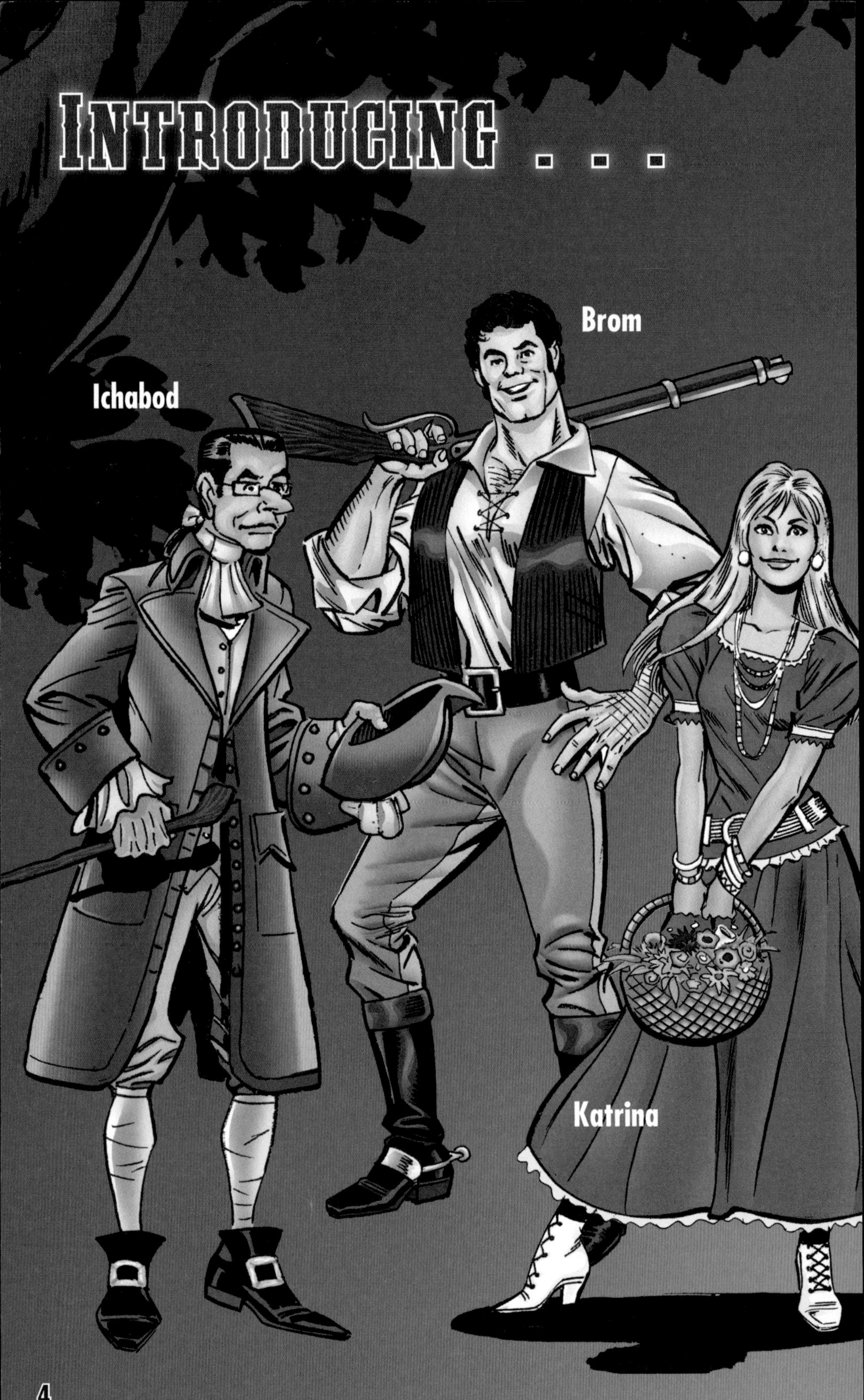

INTRODUCING . . .
Brom
Ichabod
Katrina

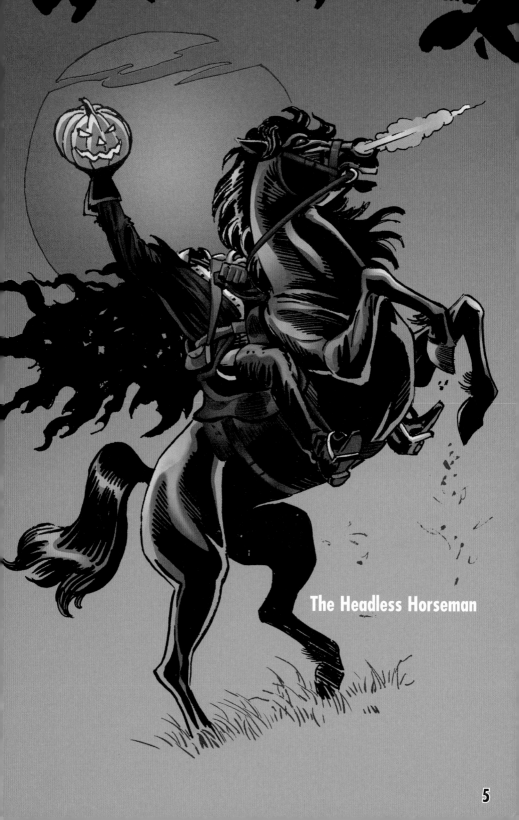

The Headless Horseman

CHAPTER 1
THE SCHOOLMASTER

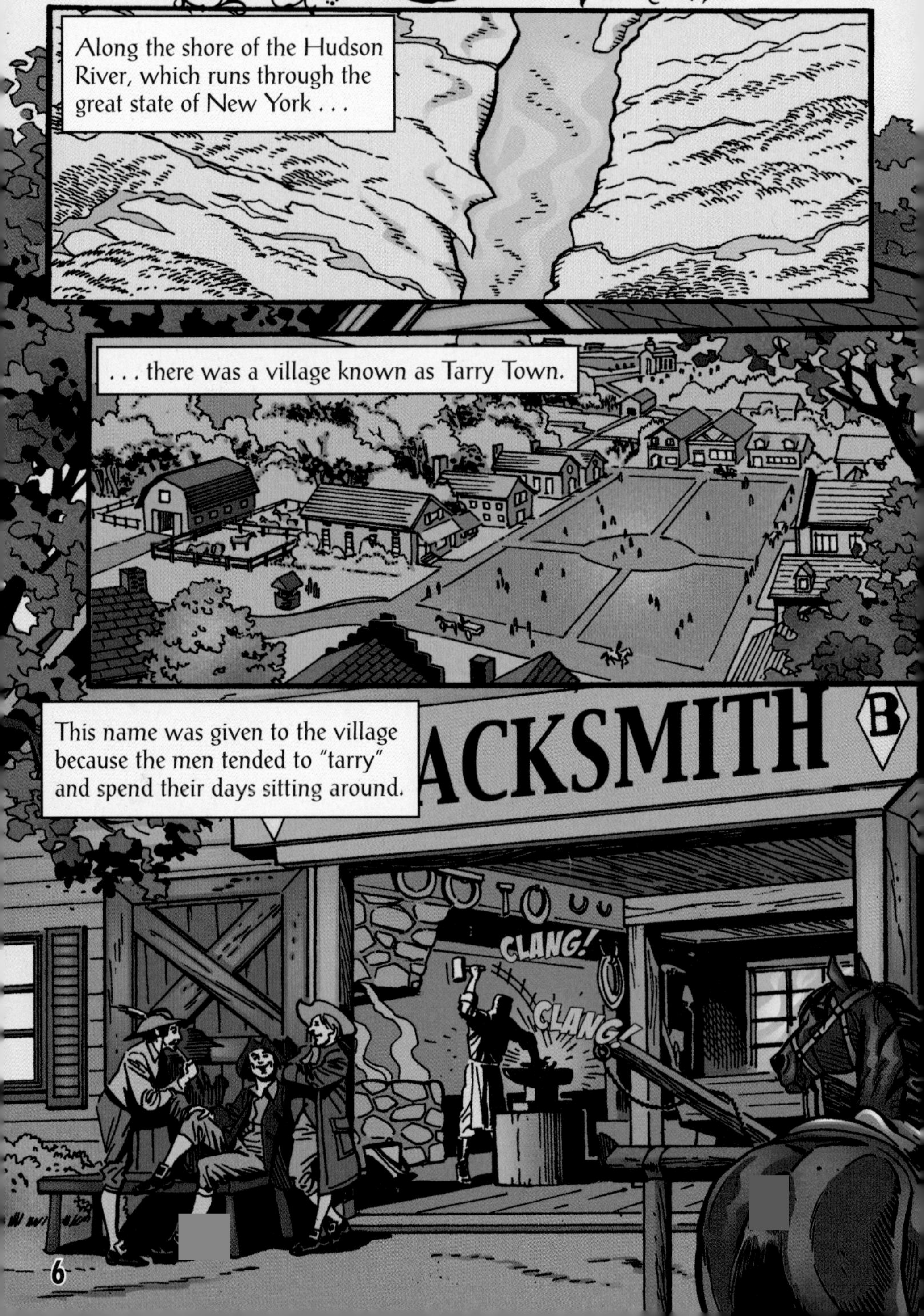
Along the shore of the Hudson River, which runs through the great state of New York . . .
. . . there was a village known as Tarry Town.
This name was given to the village because the men tended to "tarry" and spend their days sitting around.
ACKSMITH
B
CLANG!
CLANG!

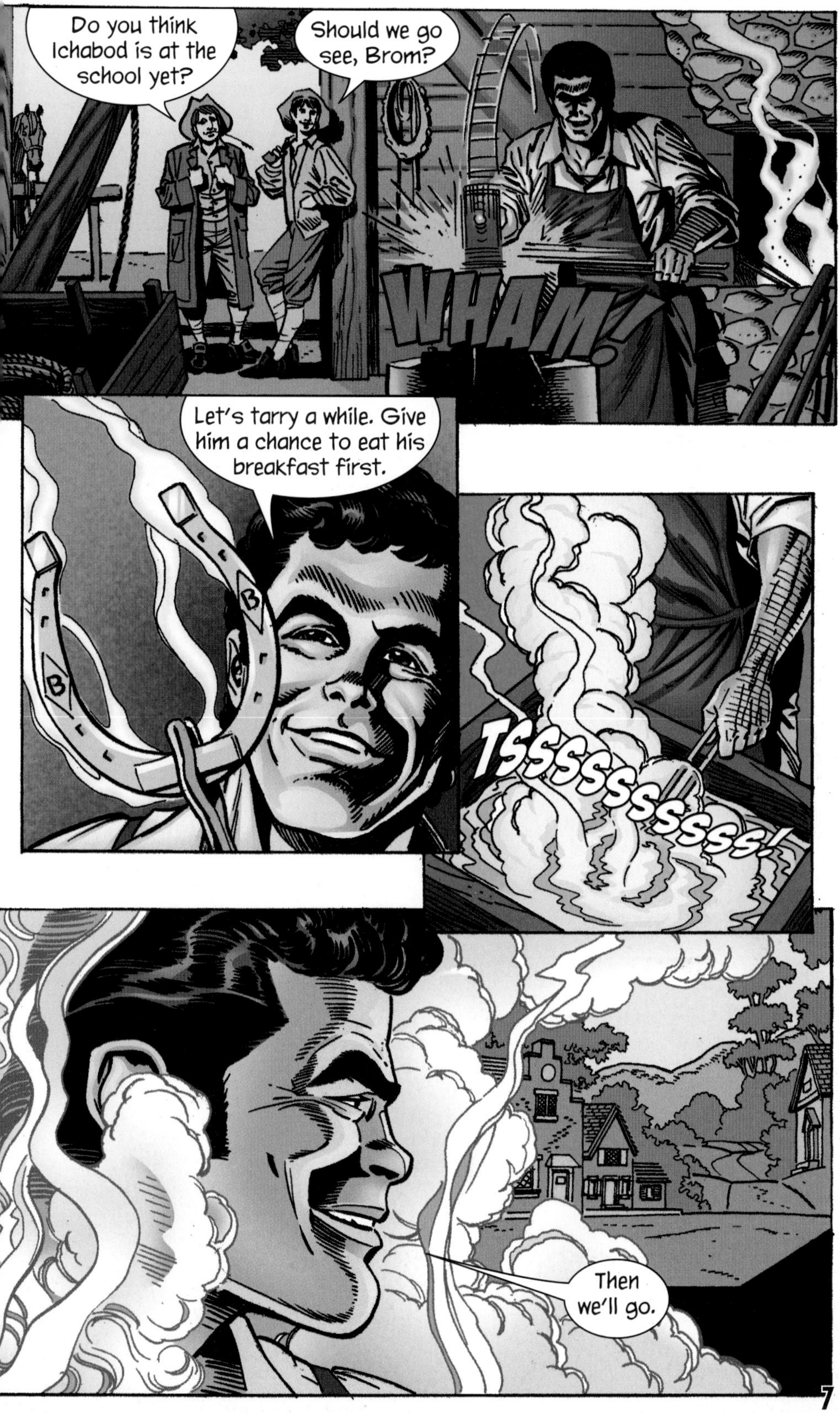
Do you think Ichabod is at the school yet?
Should we go see, Brom?
WHAM!
Let's tarry a while. Give him a chance to eat his breakfast first.
TSSSSSSSSSSSS!
Then we'll go.

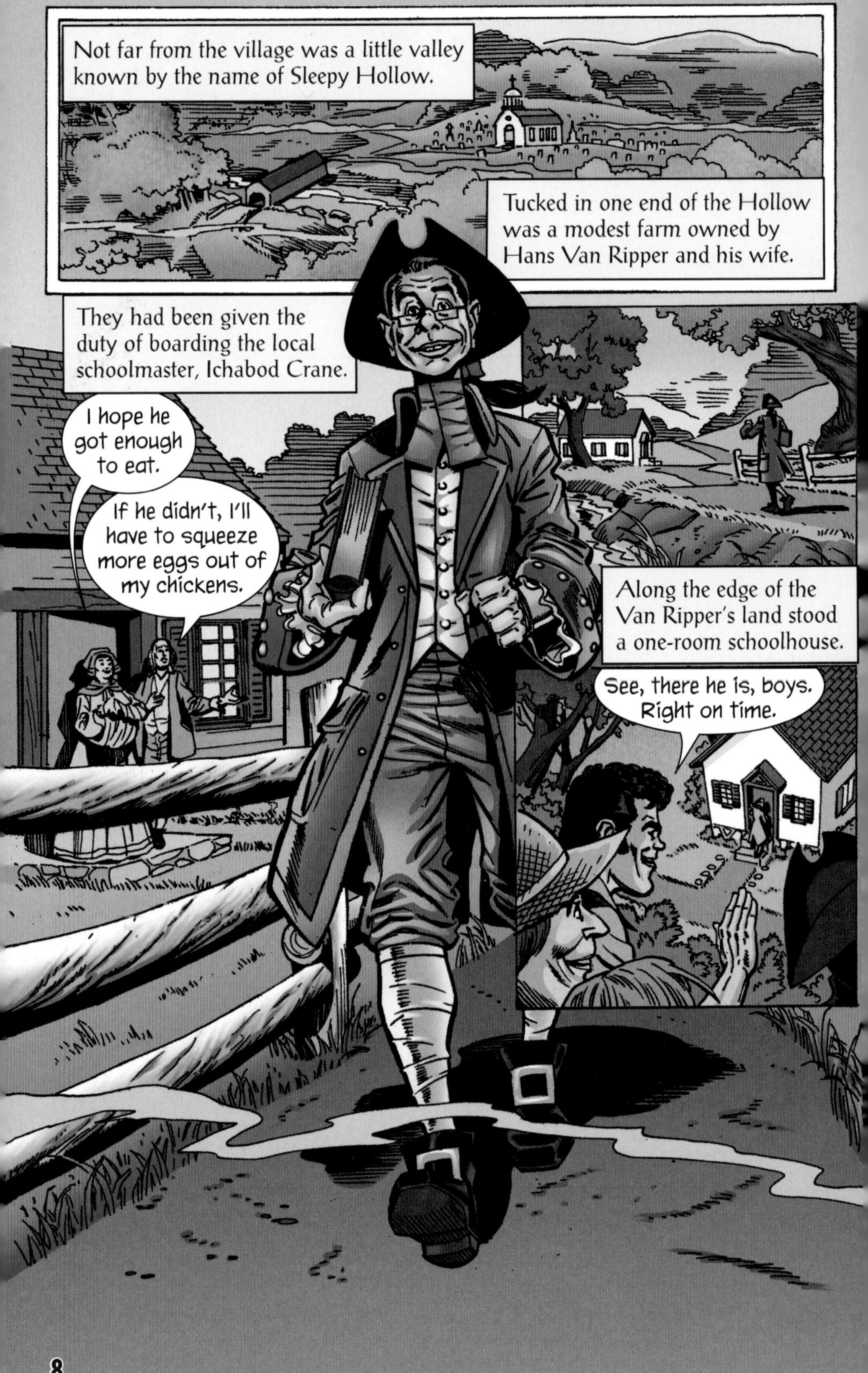
Not far from the village was a little valley known by the name of Sleepy Hollow.
Tucked in one end of the Hollow was a modest farm owned by Hans Van Ripper and his wife.
They had been given the duty of boarding the local schoolmaster, Ichabod Crane.
I hope he got enough to eat.
If he didn't, I'll have to squeeze more eggs out of my chickens.
Along the edge of the Van Ripper's land stood a one-room schoolhouse.
See, there he is, boys. Right on time.

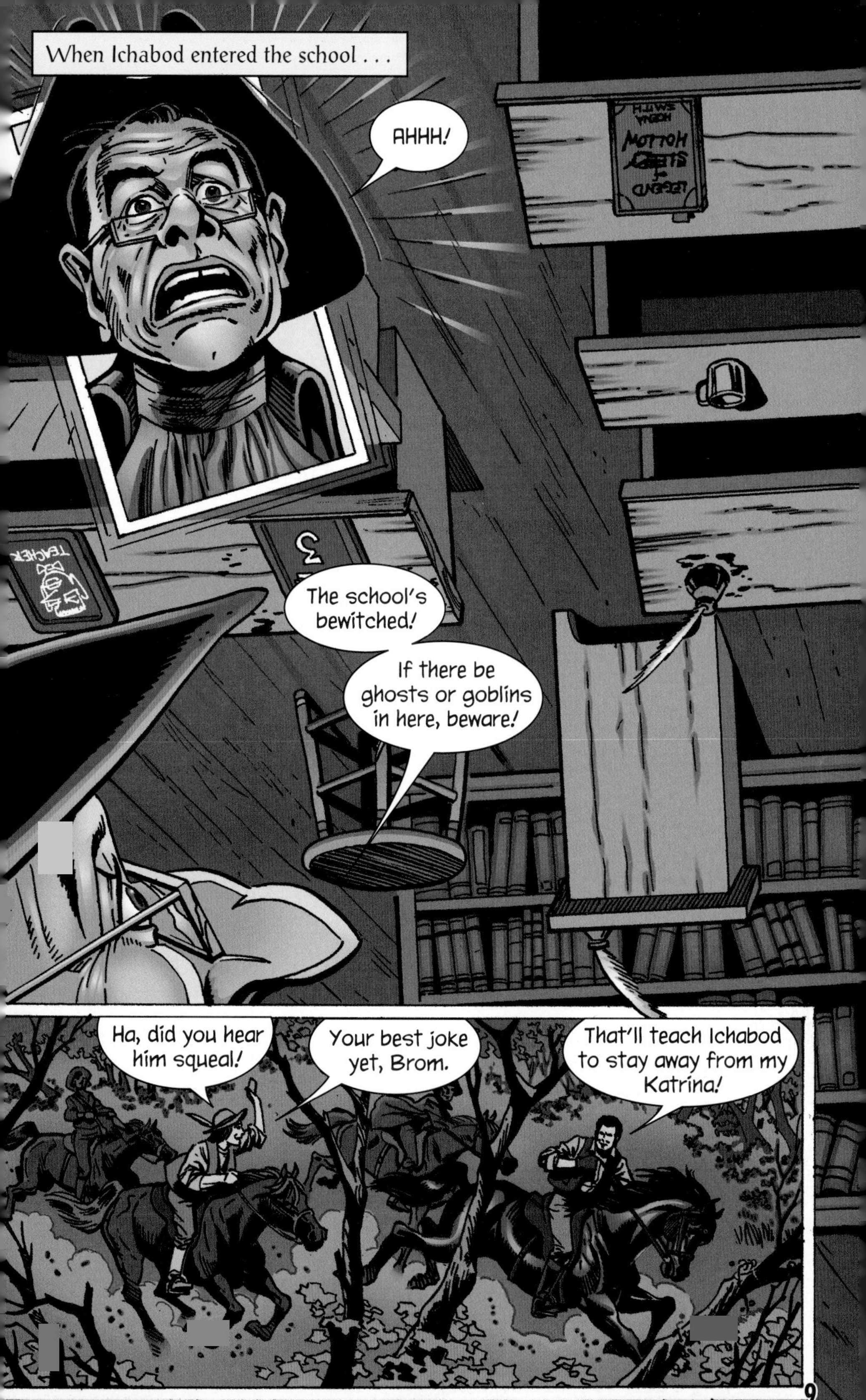
When Ichabod entered the school . . .
AHHH!
The school's bewitched!
If there be ghosts or goblins in here, beware!
Ha, did you hear him squeal!
Your best joke yet, Brom.
That'll teach Ichabod to stay away from my Katrina!

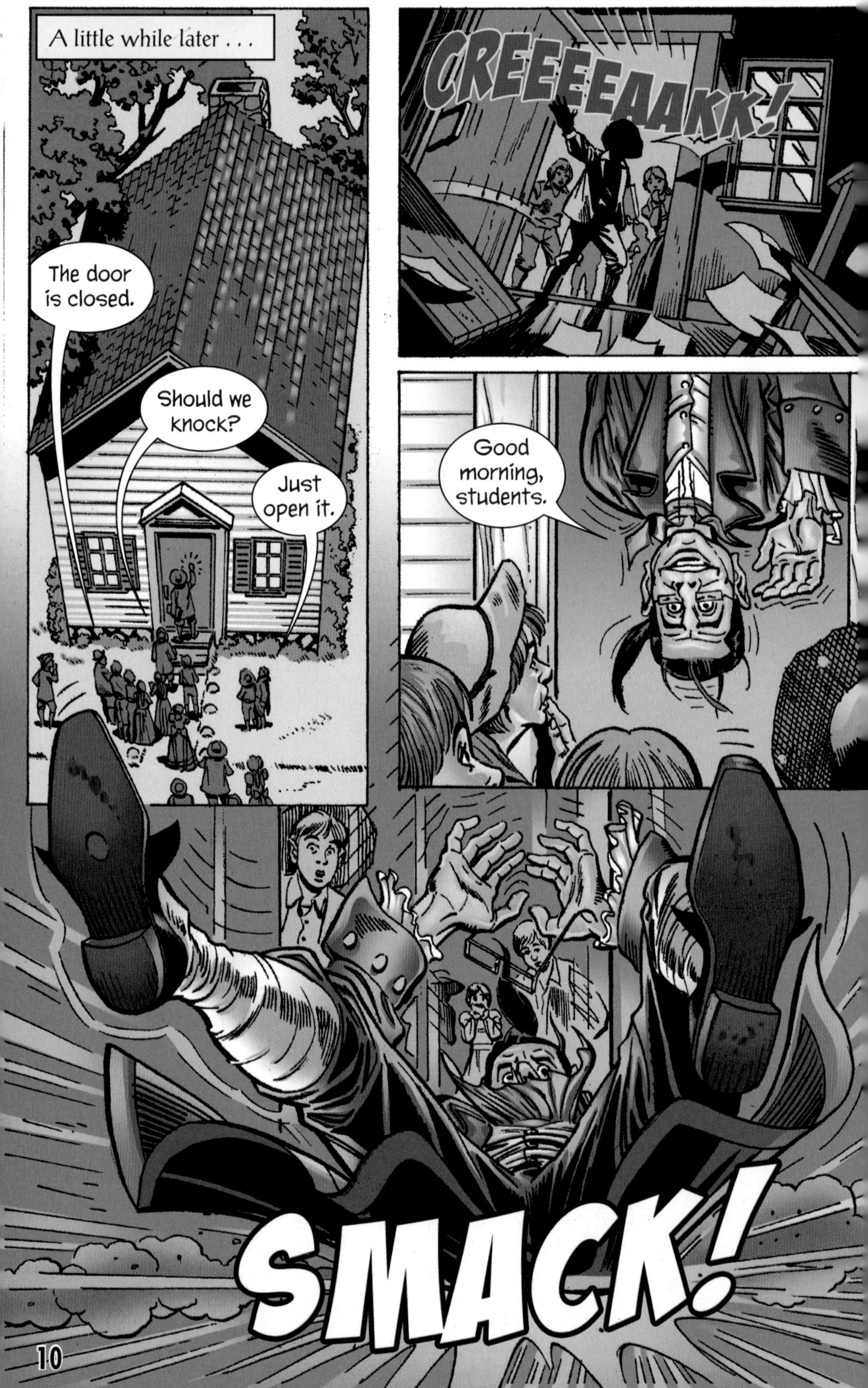
A little while later . . .
The door is closed.
Should we knock?
Just open it.
CREEEEEAAKK!
Good morning, students.
SMACK!

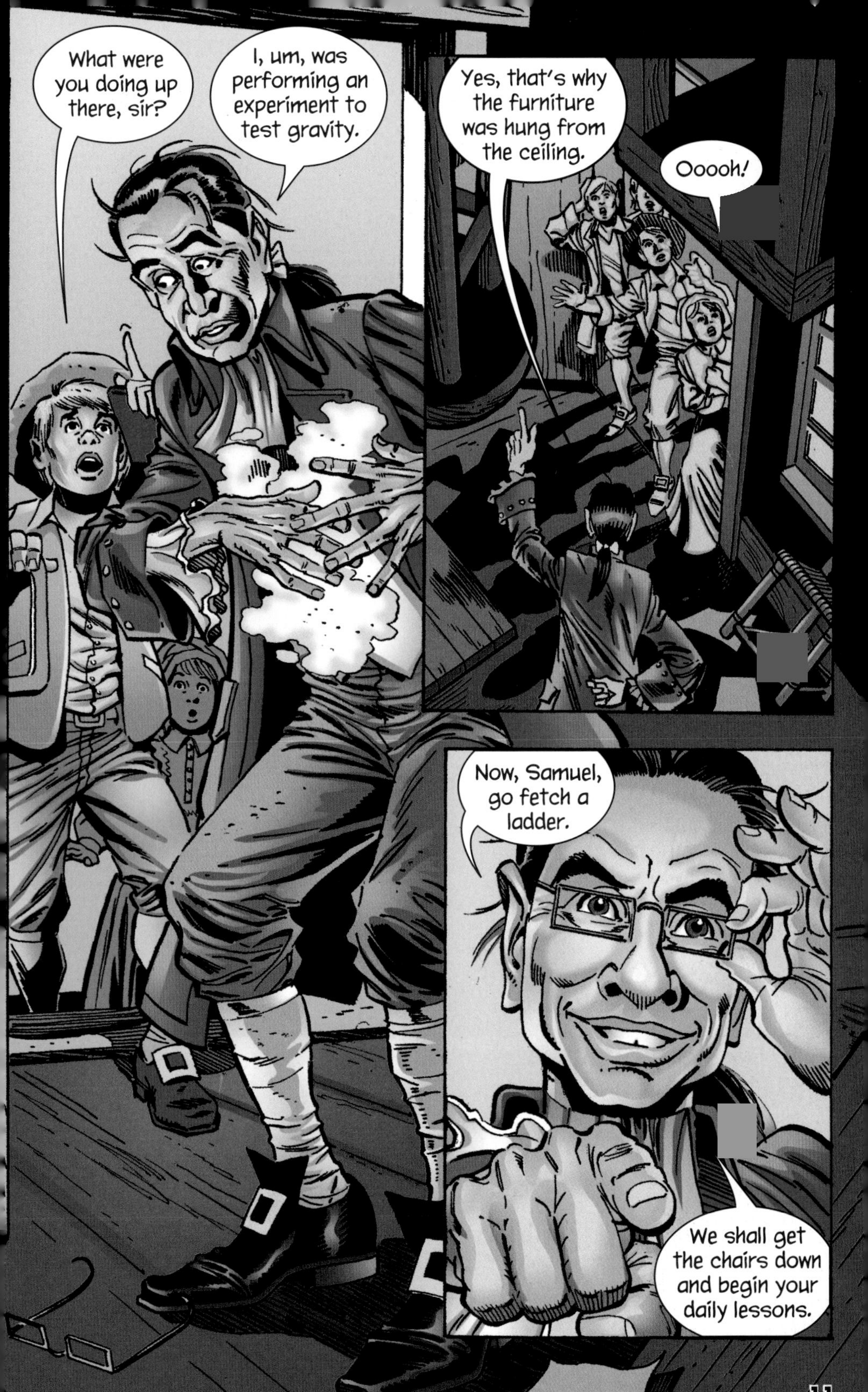
What were you doing up there, sir?
I, um, was performing an experiment to test gravity.
Yes, that's why the furniture was hung from the ceiling.
Ooooh!
Now, Samuel, go fetch a ladder.
We shall get the chairs down and begin your daily lessons.

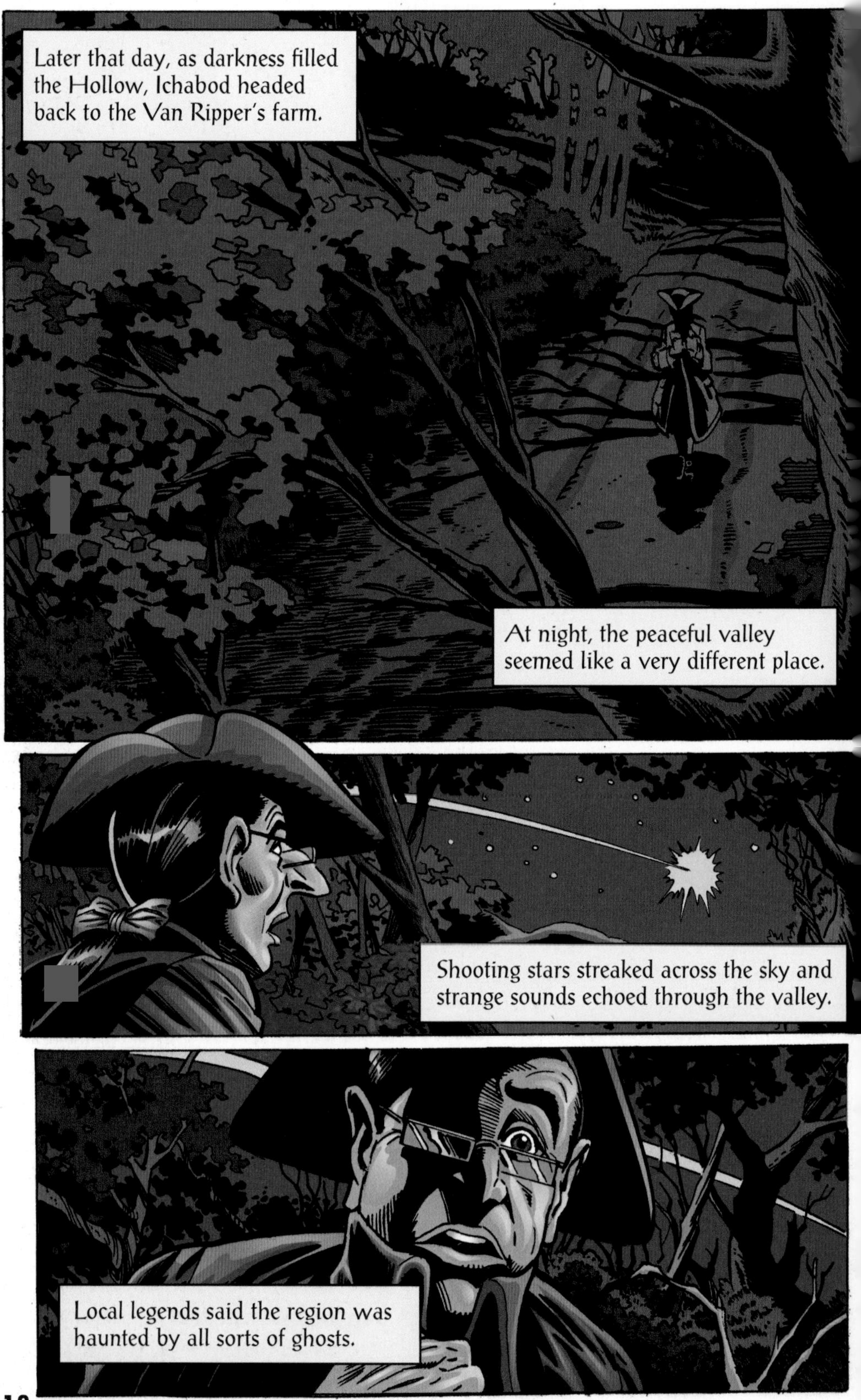
Later that day, as darkness filled the Hollow, Ichabod headed back to the Van Ripper's farm.
At night, the peaceful valley seemed like a very different place.
Shooting stars streaked across the sky and strange sounds echoed through the valley.
Local legends said the region was haunted by all sorts of ghosts.

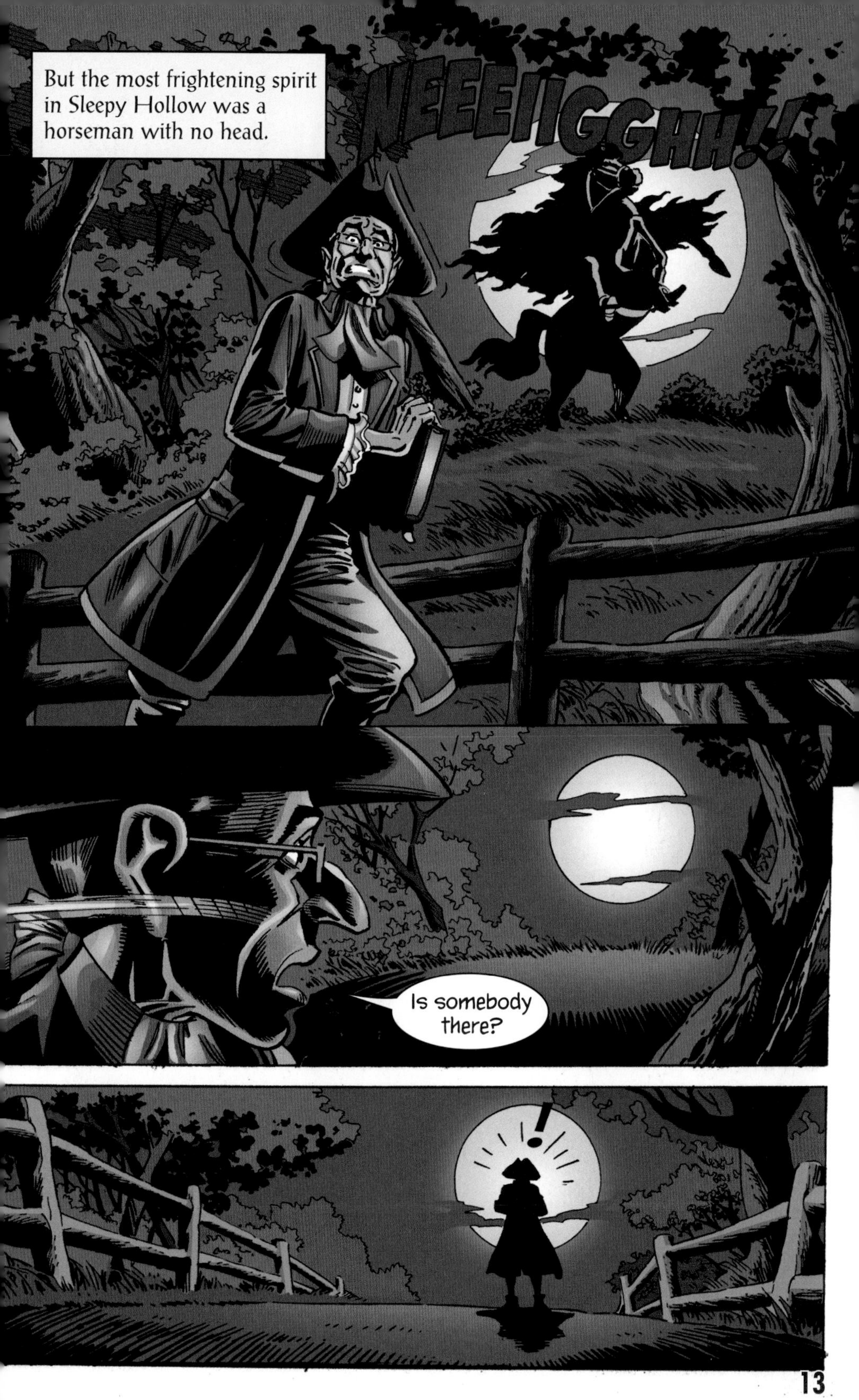
But the most frightening spirit in Sleepy Hollow was a horseman with no head.
NEEEIIGGHH!!!
Is somebody there?
!

CHAPTER 2
A GHOST STORY

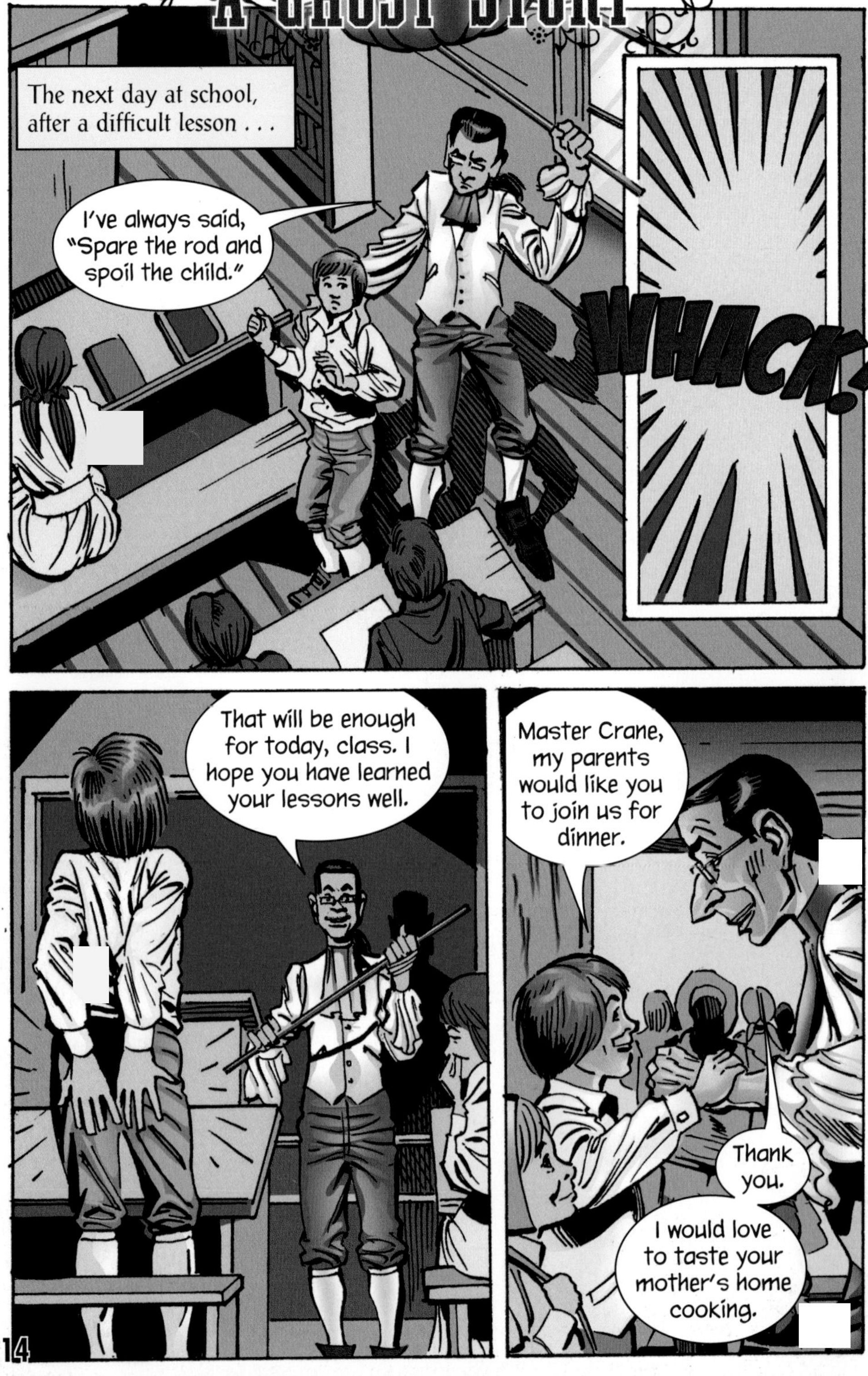
The next day at school, after a difficult lesson . . .
I've always said, "Spare the rod and spoil the child."
WHACK!
That will be enough for today, class. I hope you have learned your lessons well.
Master Crane, my parents would like you to join us for dinner.
Thank you.
I would love to taste your mother's home cooking.

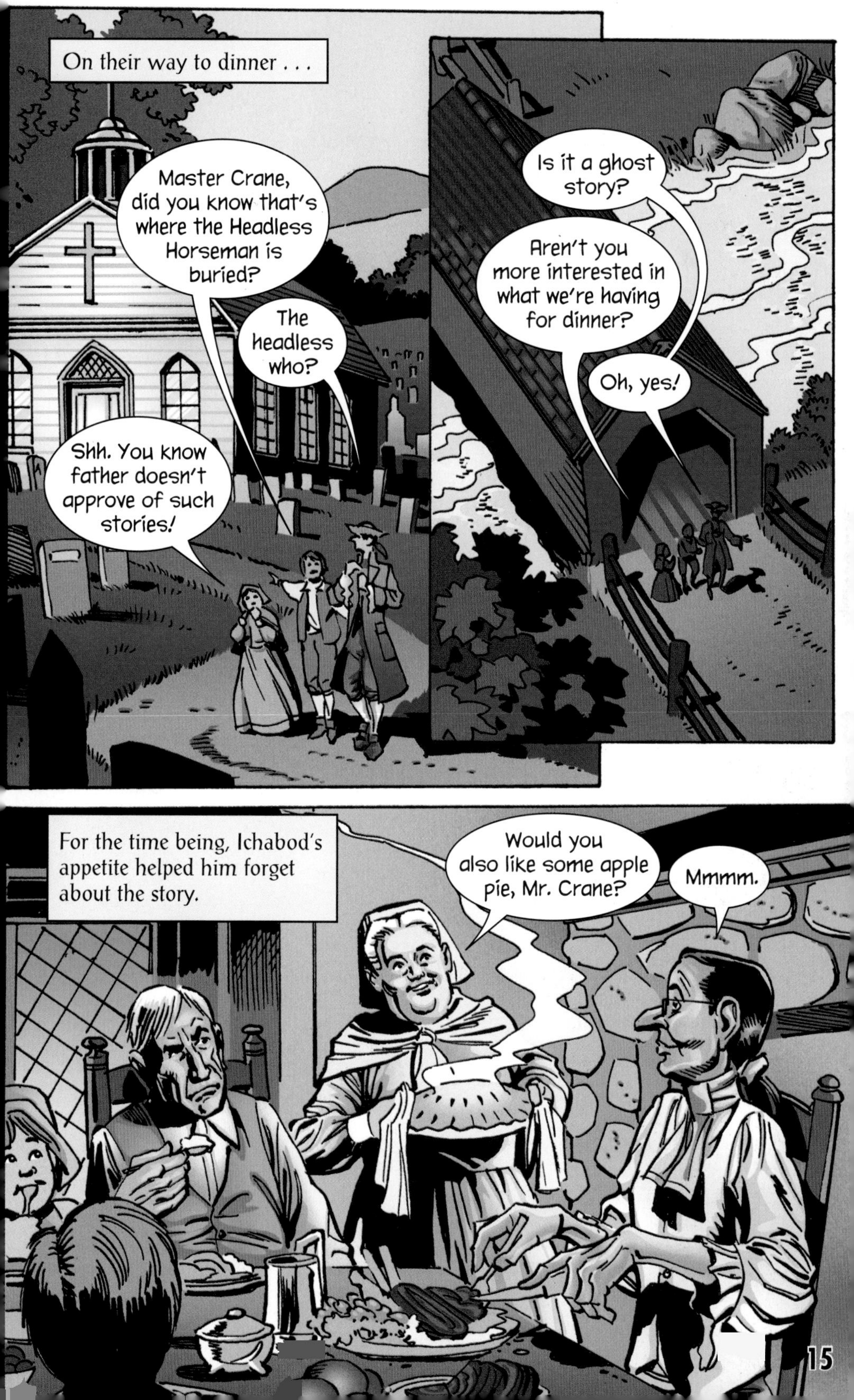
On their way to dinner . . .
Master Crane, did you know that's where the Headless Horseman is buried?
The headless who?
Shh. You know father doesn't approve of such stories!
Is it a ghost story?
Aren't you more interested in what we're having for dinner?
Oh, yes!
For the time being, Ichabod's appetite helped him forget about the story.
Would you also like some apple pie, Mr. Crane?
Mmmm.

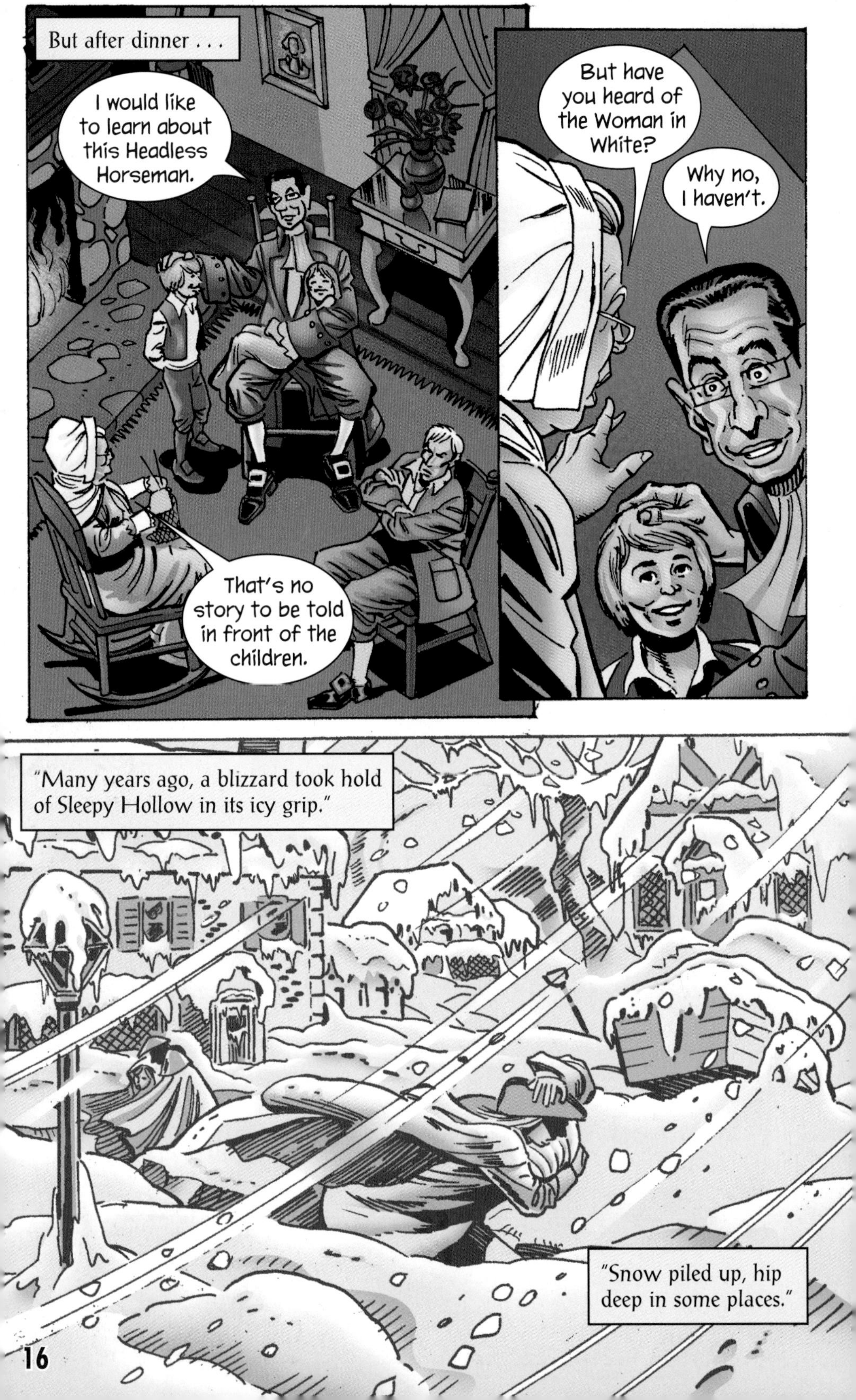
But after dinner . . .
I would like to learn about this Headless Horseman.
That's no story to be told in front of the children.
But have you heard of the Woman in White?
Why no, I haven't.
"Many years ago, a blizzard took hold of Sleepy Hollow in its icy grip."
"Snow piled up, hip deep in some places."

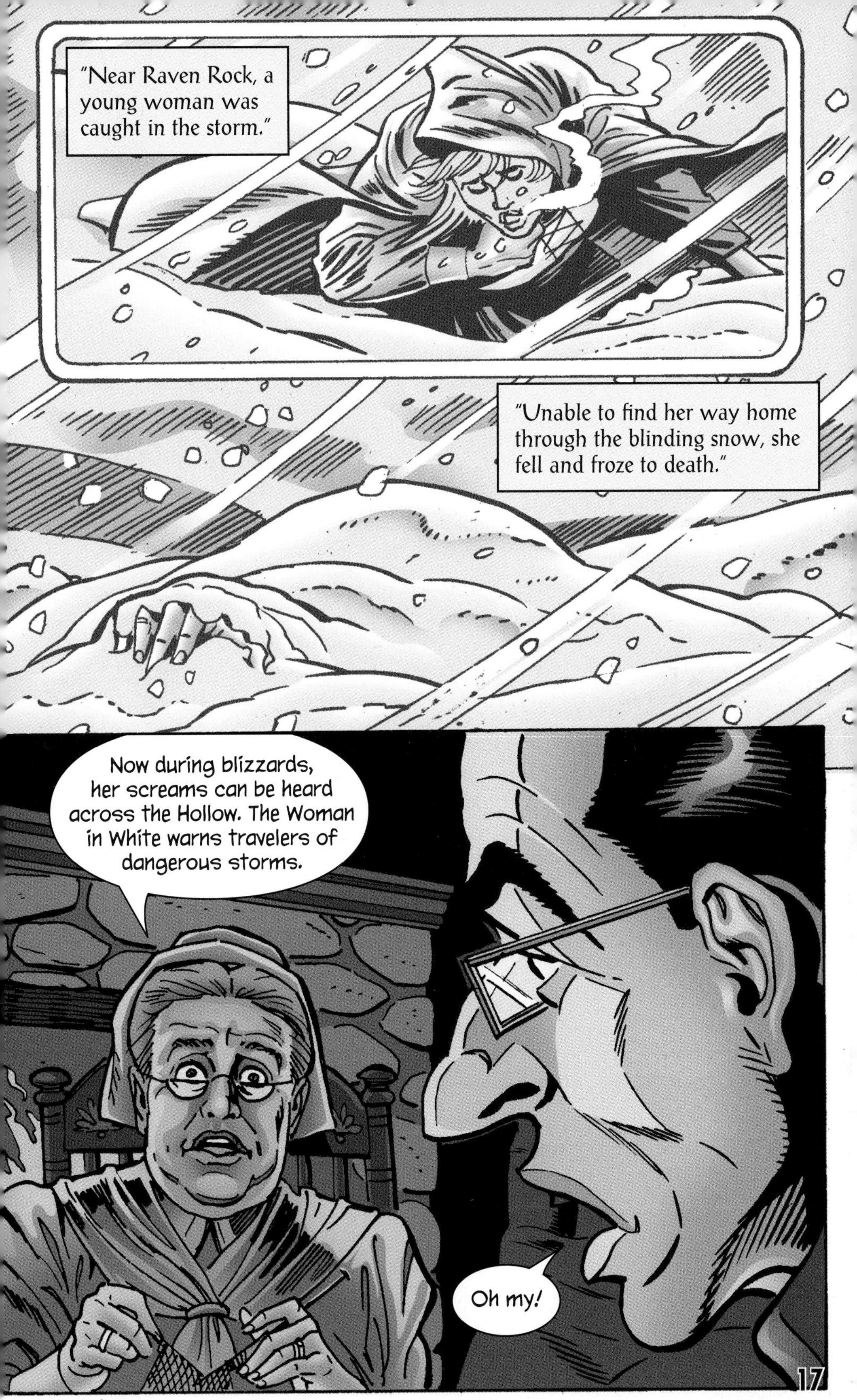
"Near Raven Rock, a young woman was caught in the storm."
"Unable to find her way home through the blinding snow, she fell and froze to death."
Now during blizzards, her screams can be heard across the Hollow. The Woman in White warns travelers of dangerous storms.
Oh my!

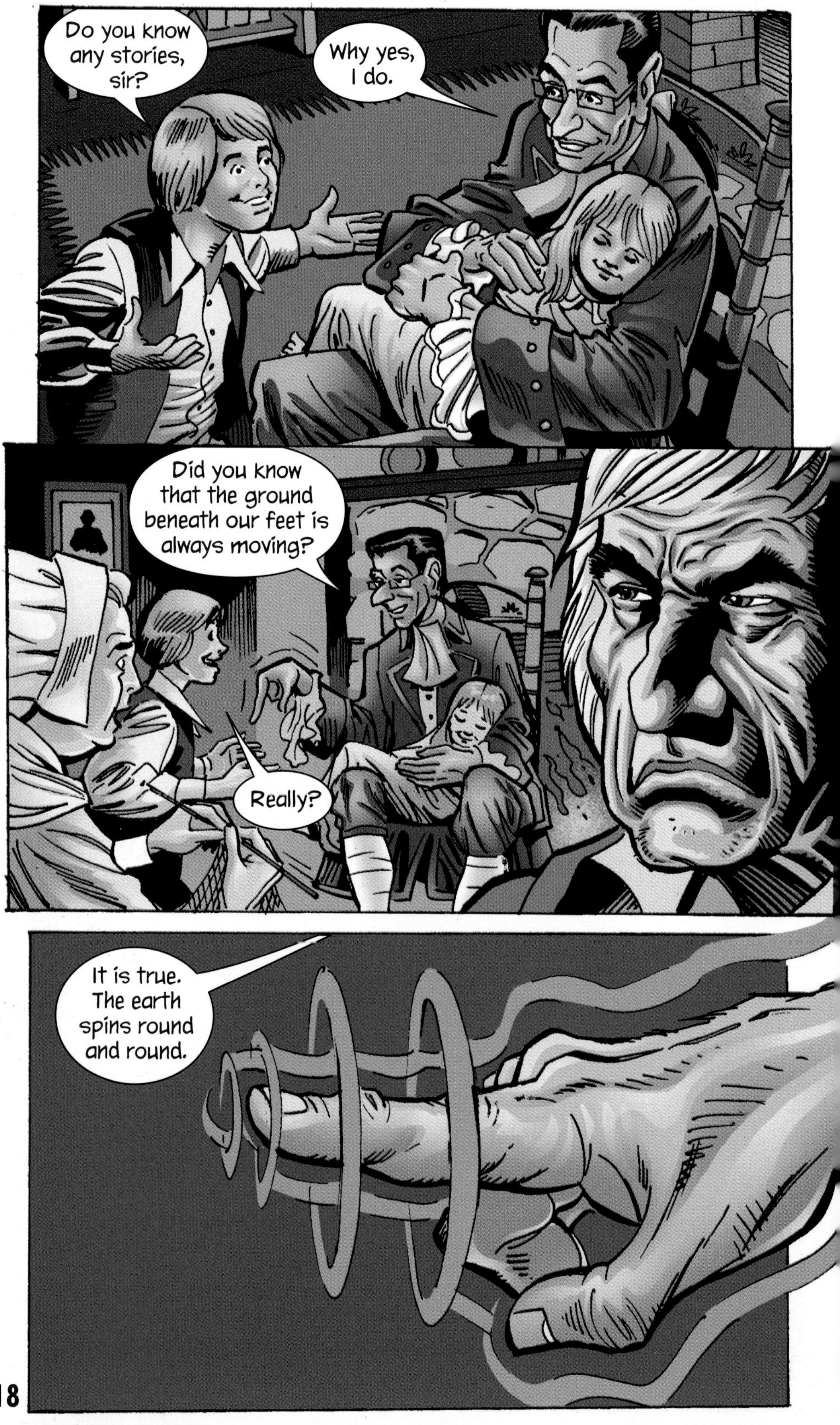
Do you know any stories, sir?
Why yes, I do.
Did you know that the ground beneath our feet is always moving?
Really?
It is true. The earth spins round and round.

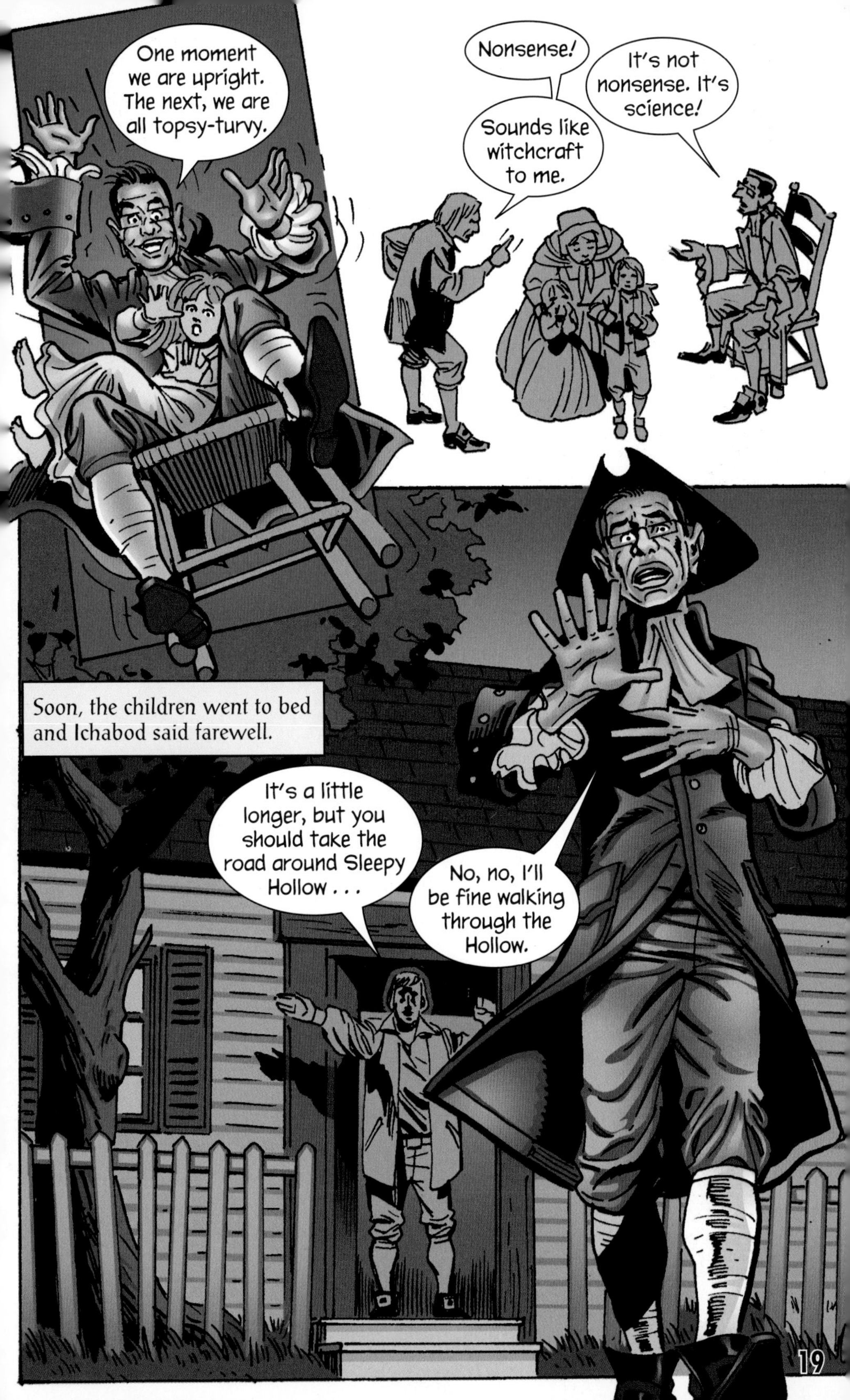
One moment we are upright. The next, we are all topsy-turvy.
Nonsense!
Sounds like witchcraft to me.
It's not nonsense. It's science!
Soon, the children went to bed and Ichabod said farewell.
It's a little longer, but you should take the road around Sleepy Hollow . . .
No, no, I'll be fine walking through the Hollow.

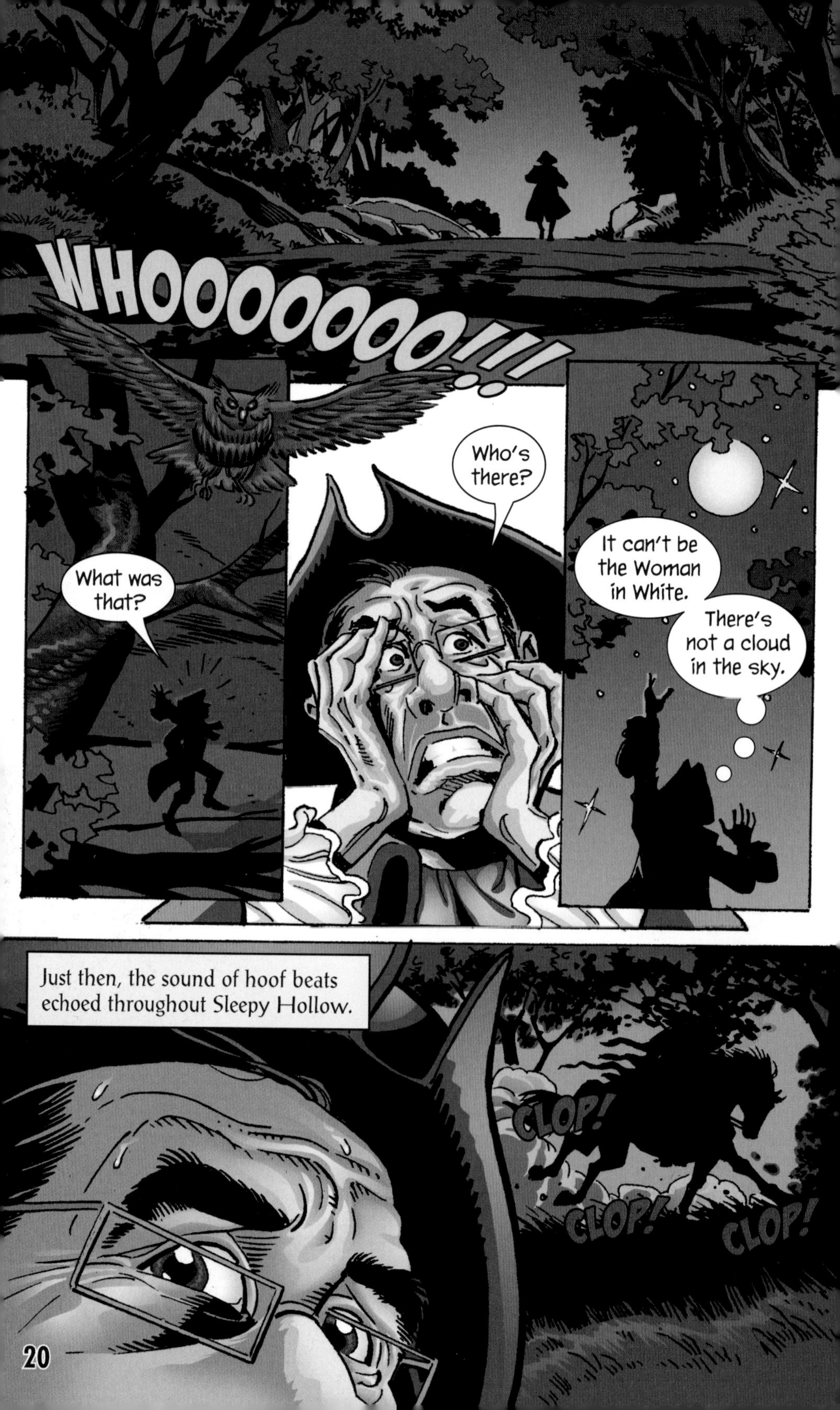
WHOOOOOOO!!!
What was that?
Who's there?
It can't be the Woman in White.
There's not a cloud in the sky.
Just then, the sound of hoof beats echoed throughout Sleepy Hollow.
CLOP!
CLOP!
CLOP!

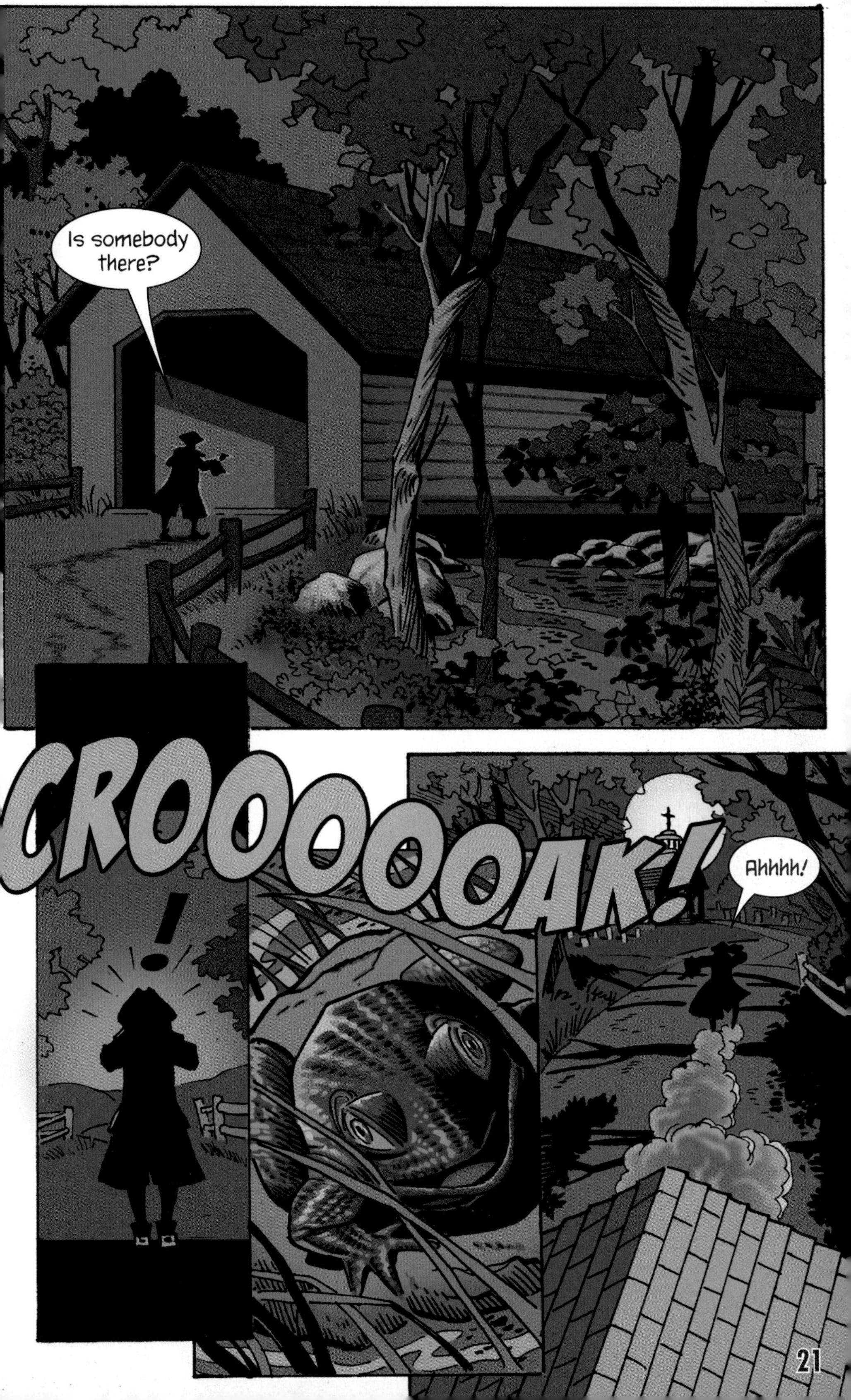
Is somebody there?
CROOOOOAK!
!
Ahhhh!

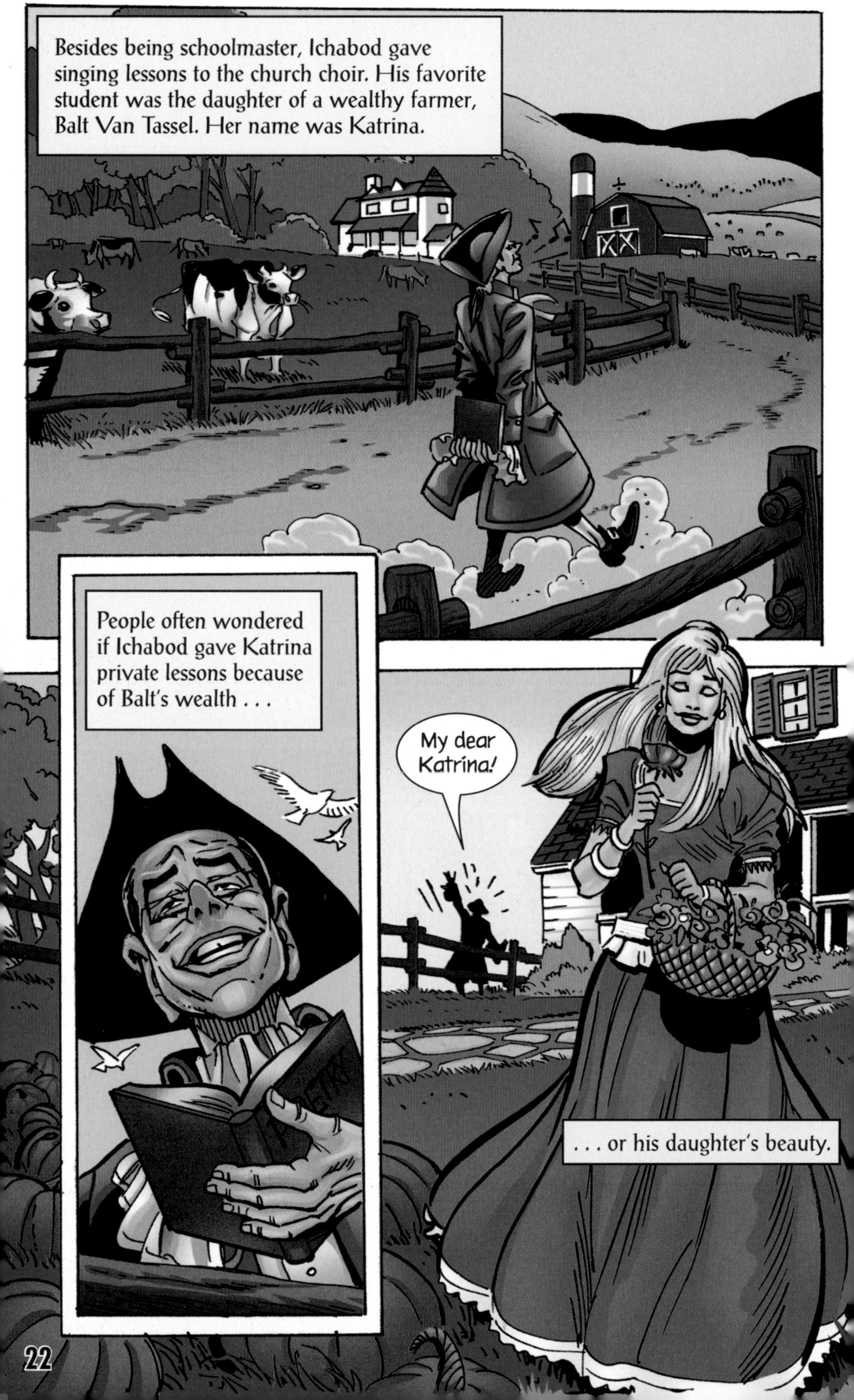
Besides being schoolmaster, Ichabod gave singing lessons to the church choir. His favorite student was the daughter of a wealthy farmer, Balt Van Tassel. Her name was Katrina.
People often wondered if Ichabod gave Katrina private lessons because of Balt's wealth . . .
My dear Katrina!
. . . or his daughter's beauty.

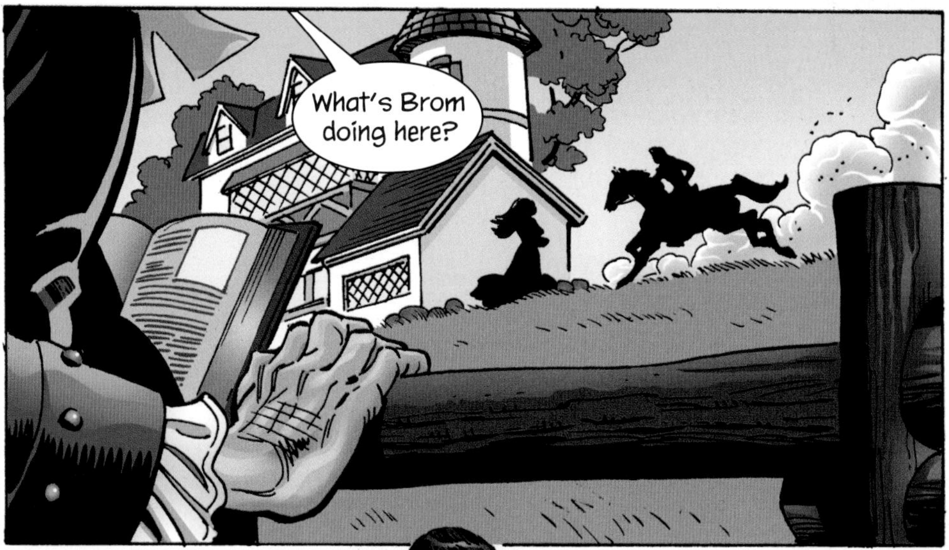
What's Brom doing here?

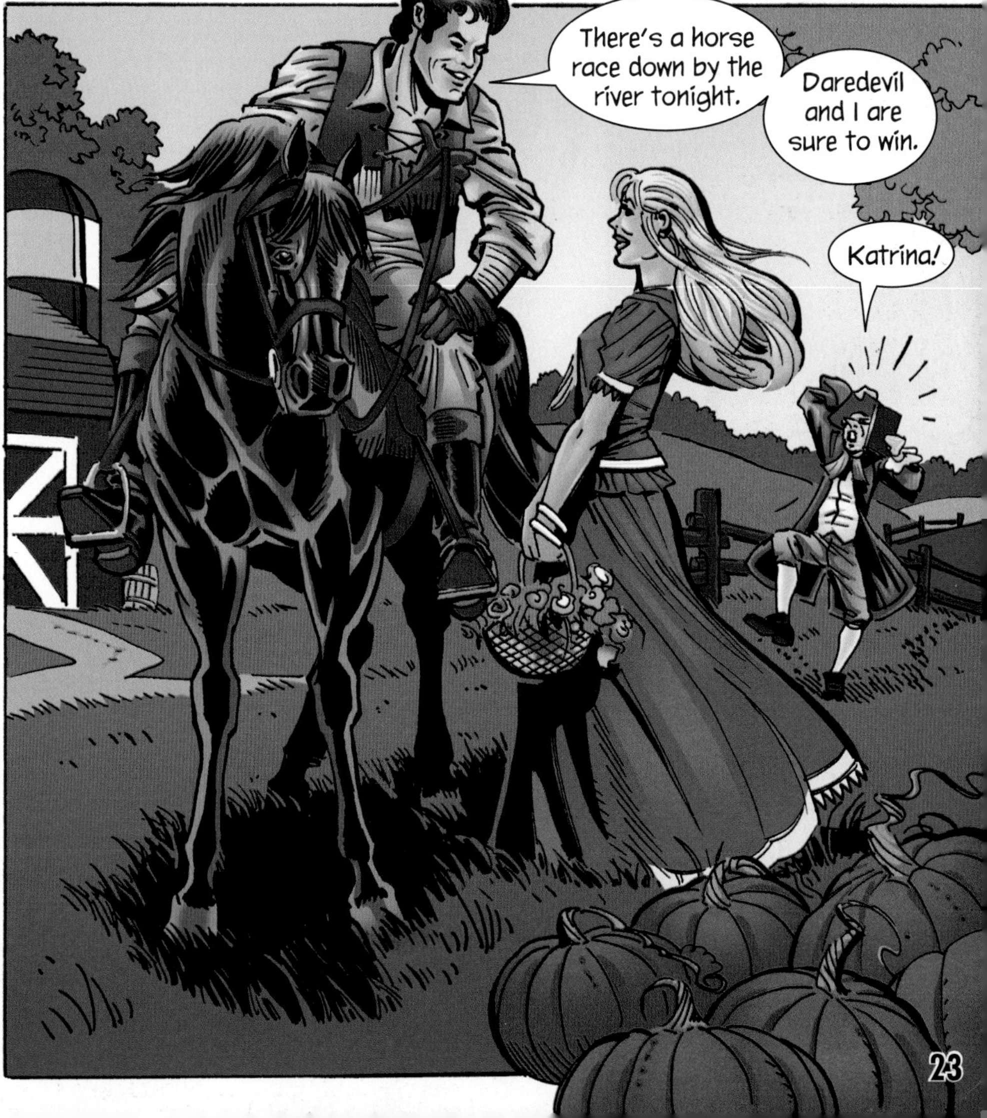
There's a horse race down by the river tonight.
Daredevil and I are sure to win.
Katrina!

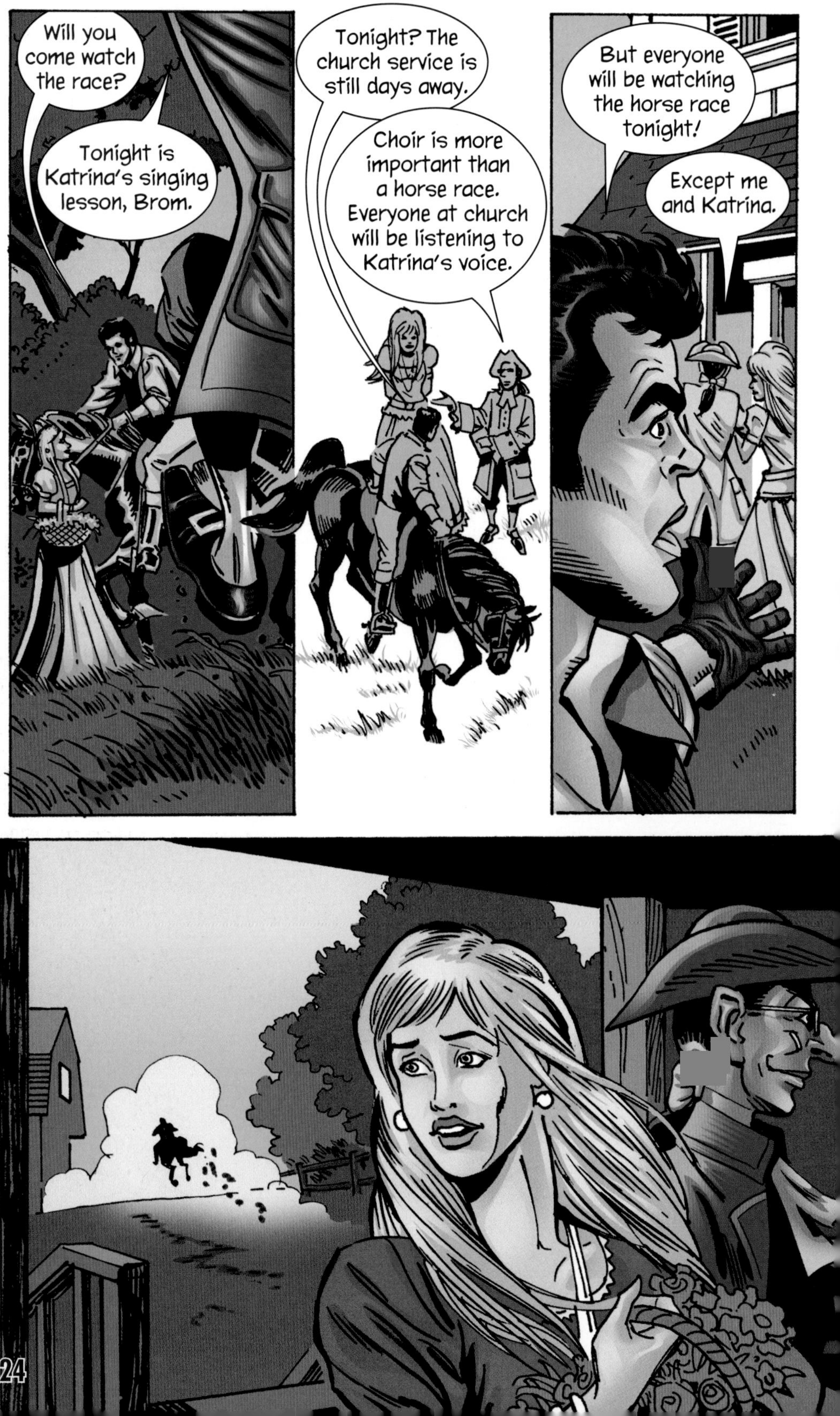
Will you come watch the race?
Tonight is Katrina's singing lesson, Brom.
Tonight? The church service is still days away.
Choir is more important than a horse race. Everyone at church will be listening to Katrina's voice.
But everyone will be watching the horse race tonight!
Except me and Katrina.

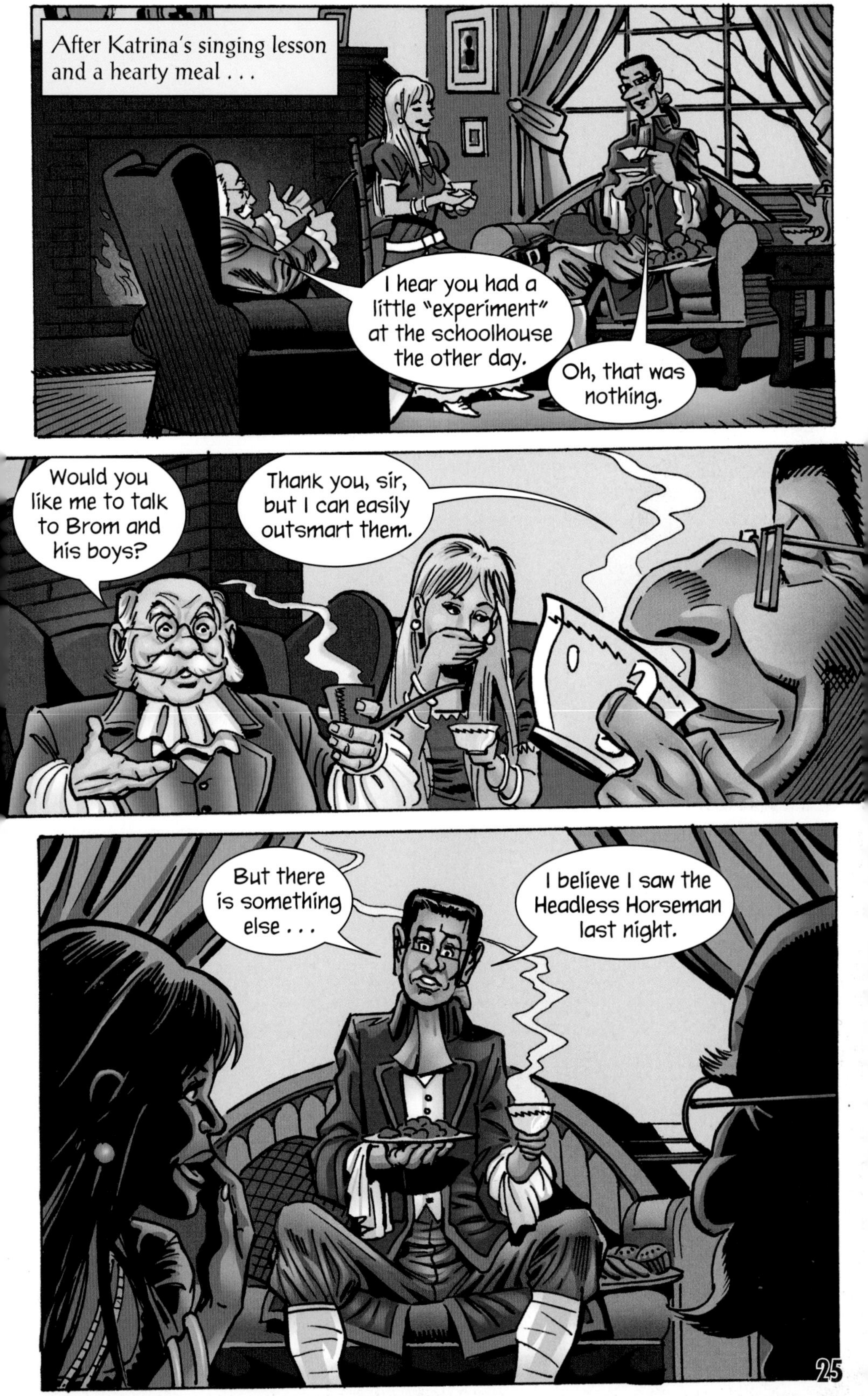
After Katrina's singing lesson and a hearty meal . . .
I hear you had a little "experiment" at the schoolhouse the other day.
Oh, that was nothing.
Would you like me to talk to Brom and his boys?
Thank you, sir, but I can easily outsmart them.
But there is something else . . .
I believe I saw the Headless Horseman last night.

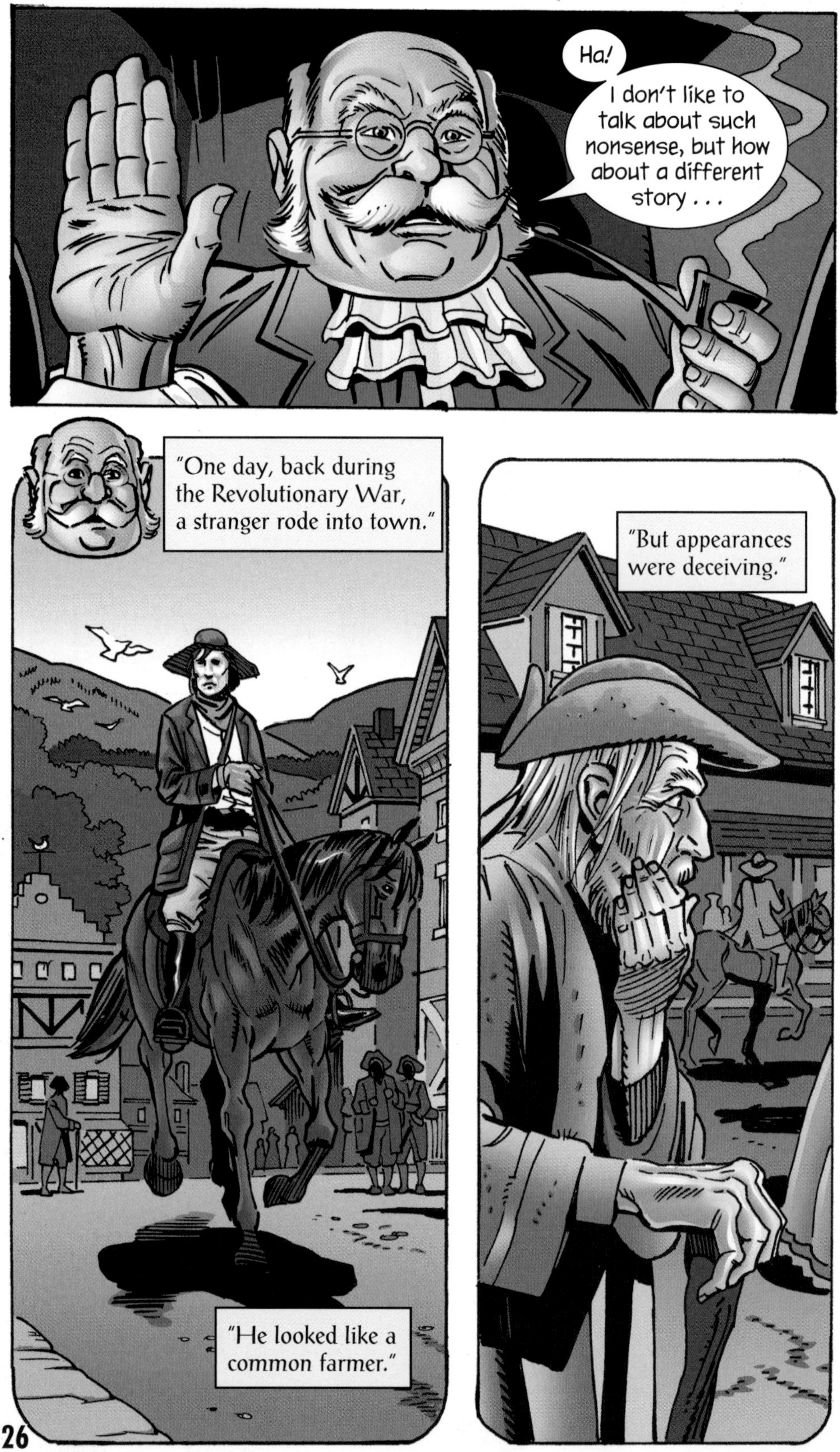
Ha!
I don't like to talk about such nonsense, but how about a different story . . .
"One day, back during the Revolutionary War, a stranger rode into town."
"He looked like a common farmer."
"But appearances were deceiving."

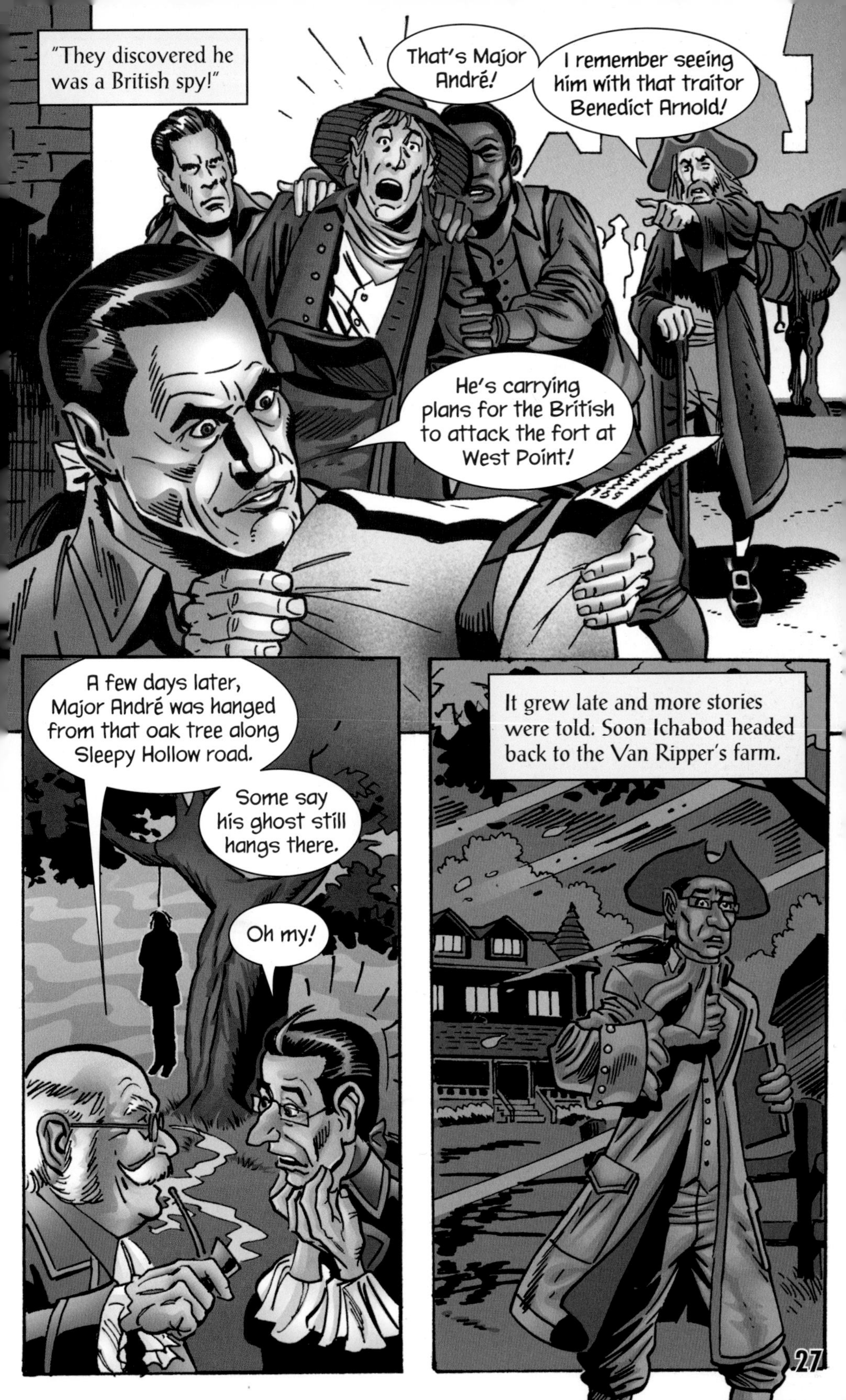

"They discovered he was a British spy!"
That's Major André!
I remember seeing him with that traitor Benedict Arnold!
He's carrying plans for the British to attack the fort at West Point!
A few days later, Major André was hanged from that oak tree along Sleepy Hollow road.
Some say his ghost still hangs there.
Oh my!
It grew late and more stories were told. Soon Ichabod headed back to the Van Ripper's farm.

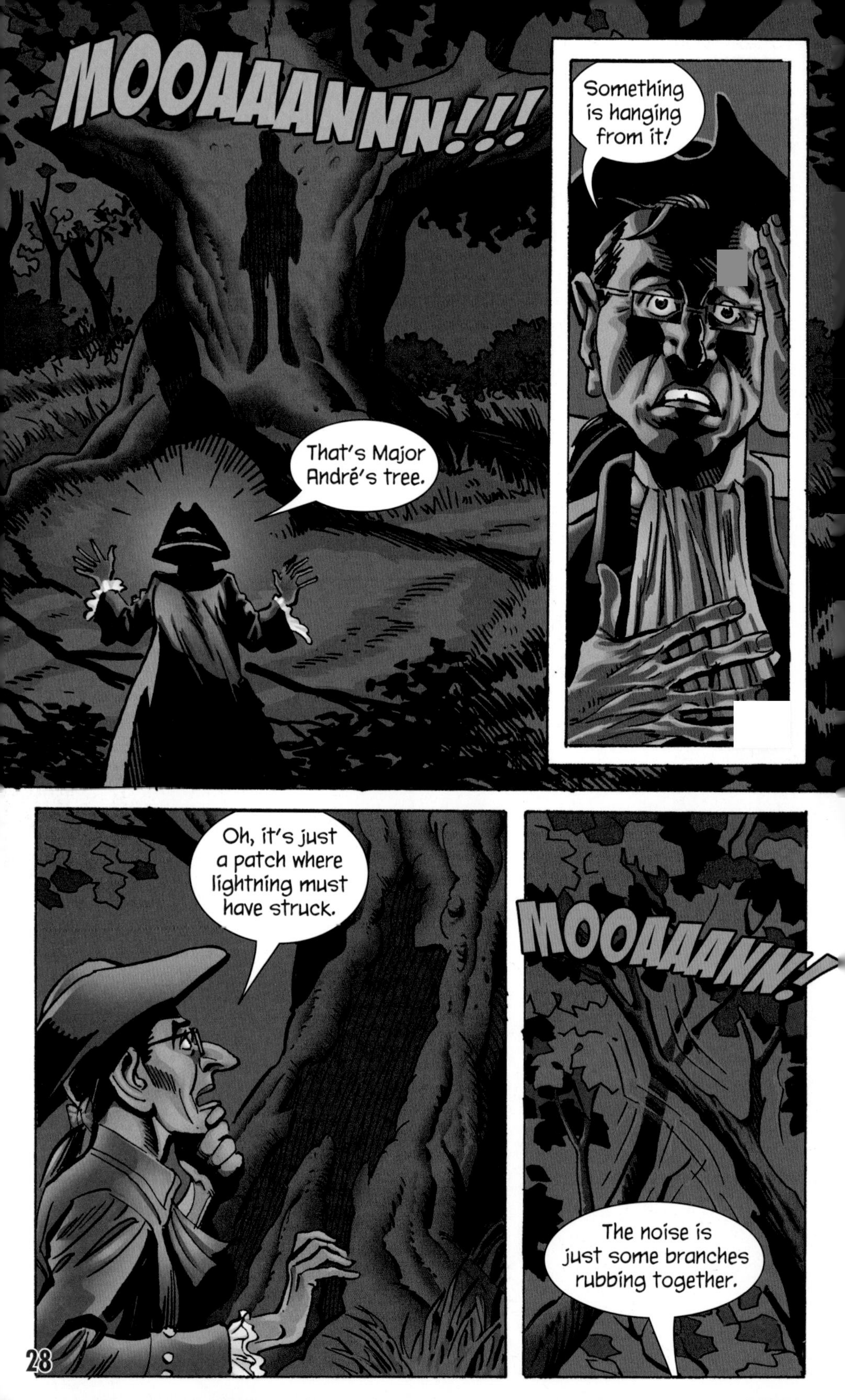
MOOAAANNN!!!
Something is hanging from it!
That's Major André's tree.
Oh, it's just a patch where lightning must have struck.
MOOAAANN!
The noise is just some branches rubbing together.

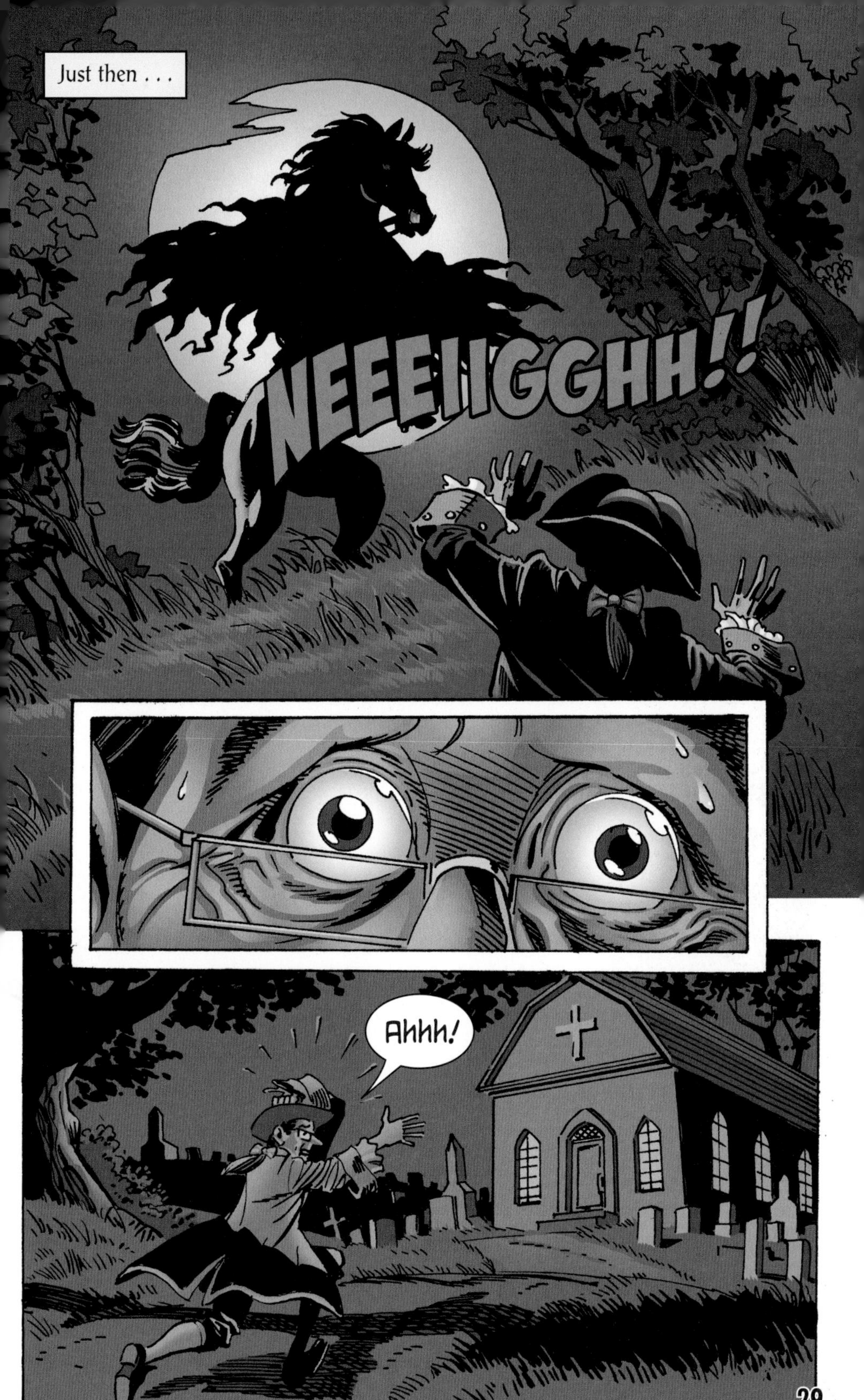
Just then . . .
NEEEIIGGHH!!
Ahhh!

CHAPTER 3
THE FINAL JOKE

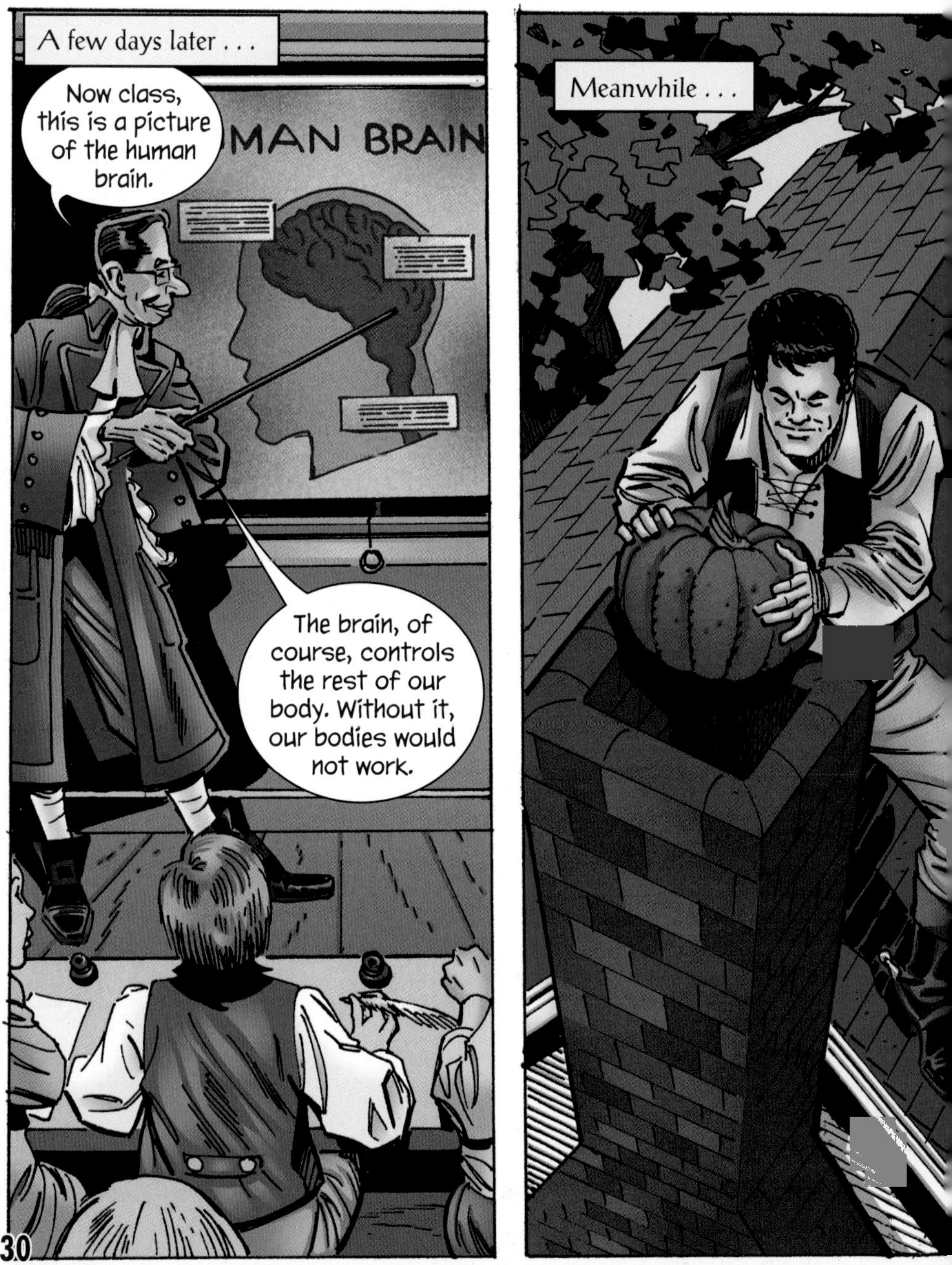
A few days later . . .
Now class, this is a picture of the human brain.
MAN BRAIN
The brain, of course, controls the rest of our body. Without it, our bodies would not work.
Meanwhile . . .

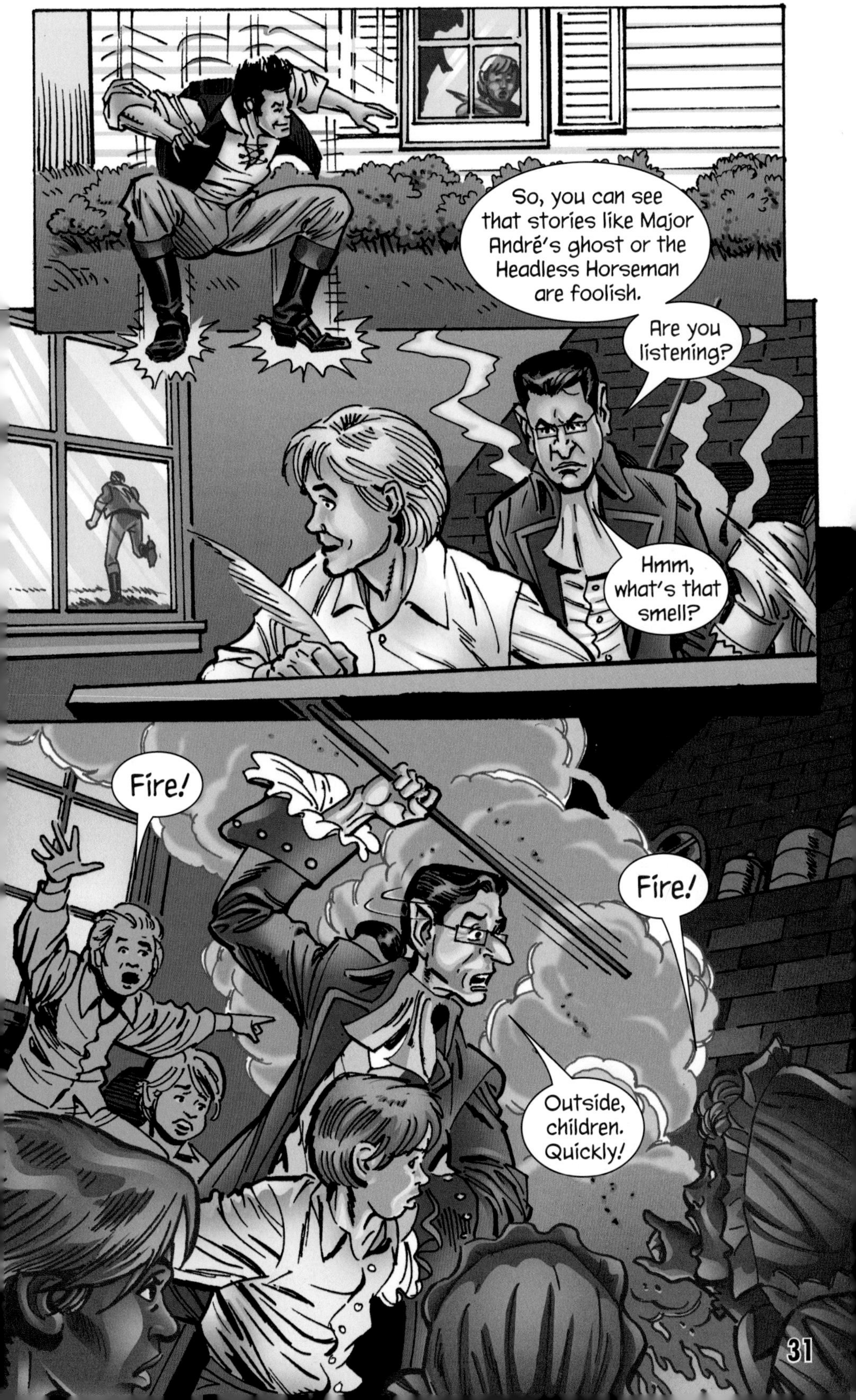
So, you can see that stories like Major André's ghost or the Headless Horseman are foolish.
Are you listening?
Hmm, what's that smell?
Fire!
Fire!
Outside, children. Quickly!

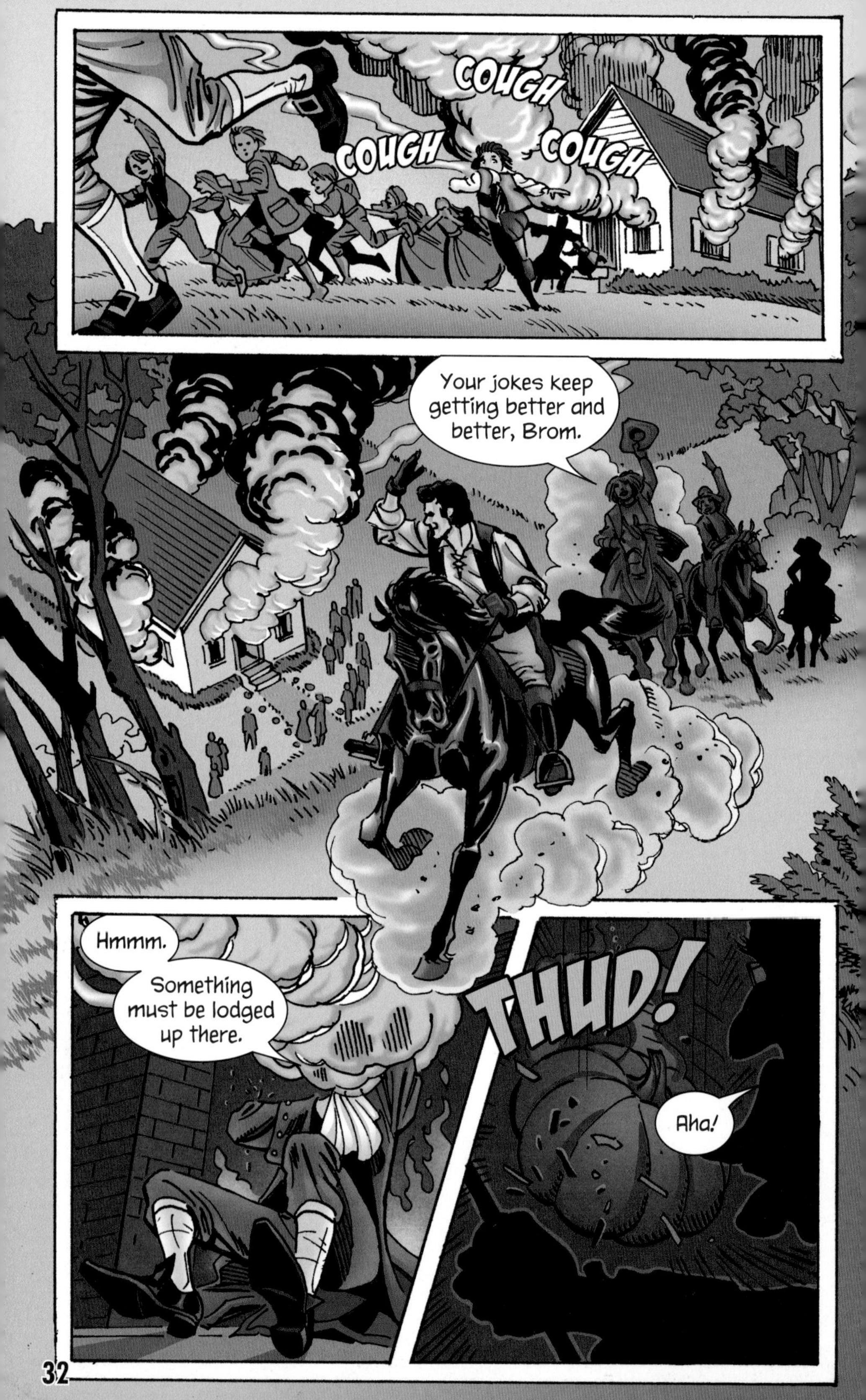
COUGH
COUGH
COUGH
Your jokes keep getting better and better, Brom.
Hmmm.
Something must be lodged up there.
THUD!
Aha!

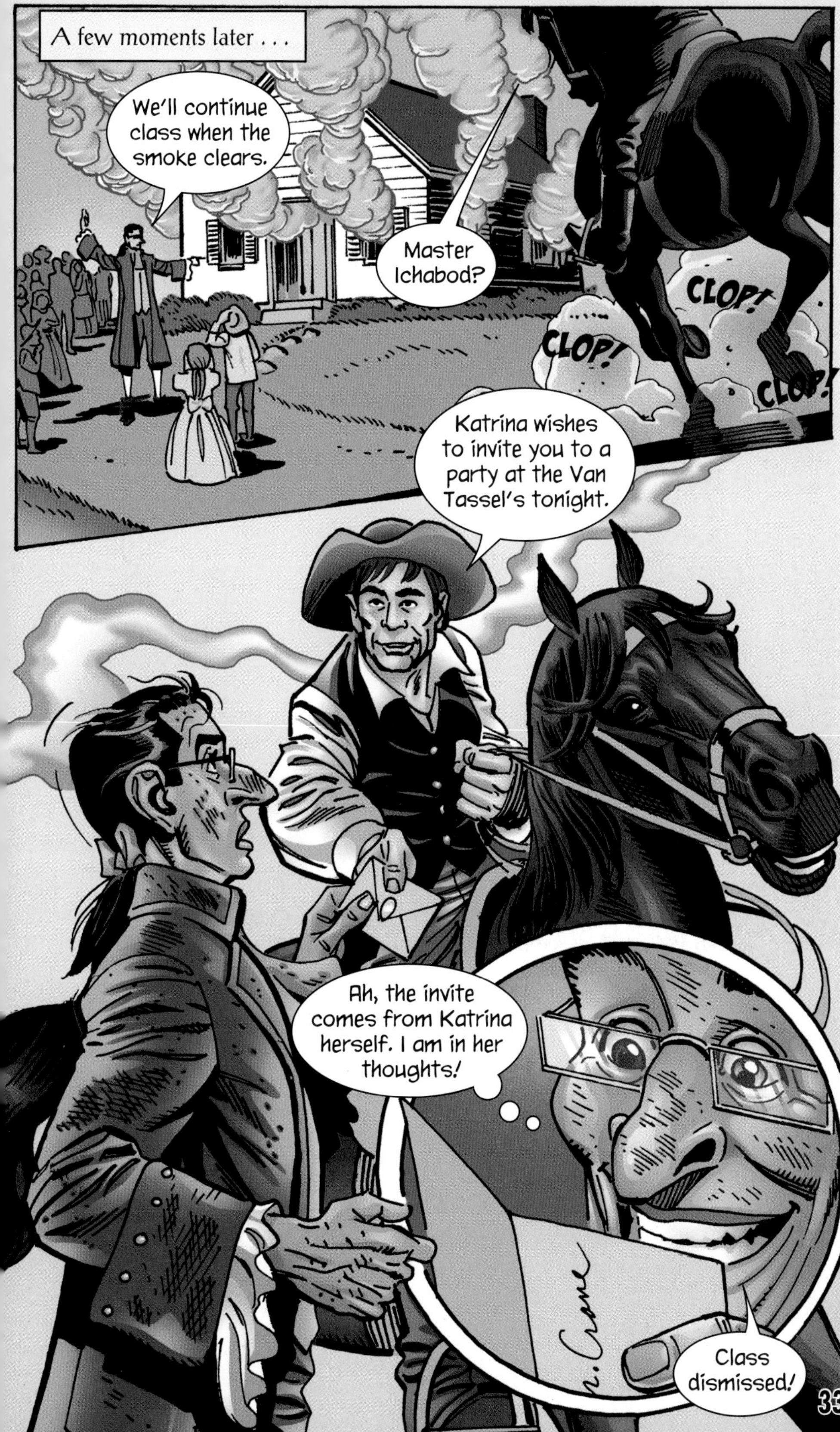
A few moments later . . .
We'll continue class when the smoke clears.
Master Ichabod?
CLOP!
CLOP!
CLOP!
Katrina wishes to invite you to a party at the Van Tassel's tonight.
Ah, the invite comes from Katrina herself. I am in her thoughts!
Class dismissed!

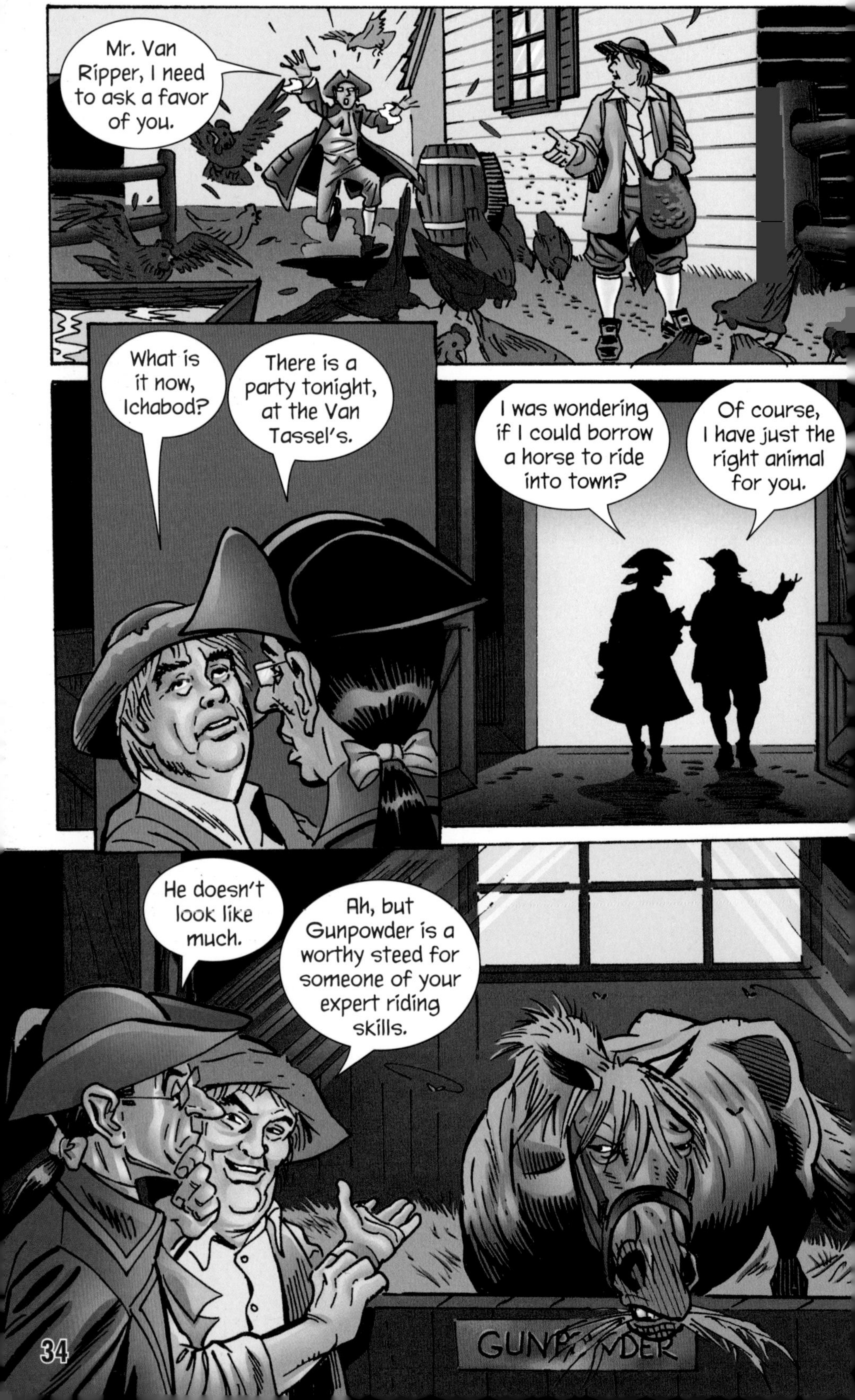
Mr. Van Ripper, I need to ask a favor of you.
What is it now, Ichabod?
There is a party tonight, at the Van Tassel's.
I was wondering if I could borrow a horse to ride into town?
Of course, I have just the right animal for you.
He doesn't look like much.
Ah, but Gunpowder is a worthy steed for someone of your expert riding skills.

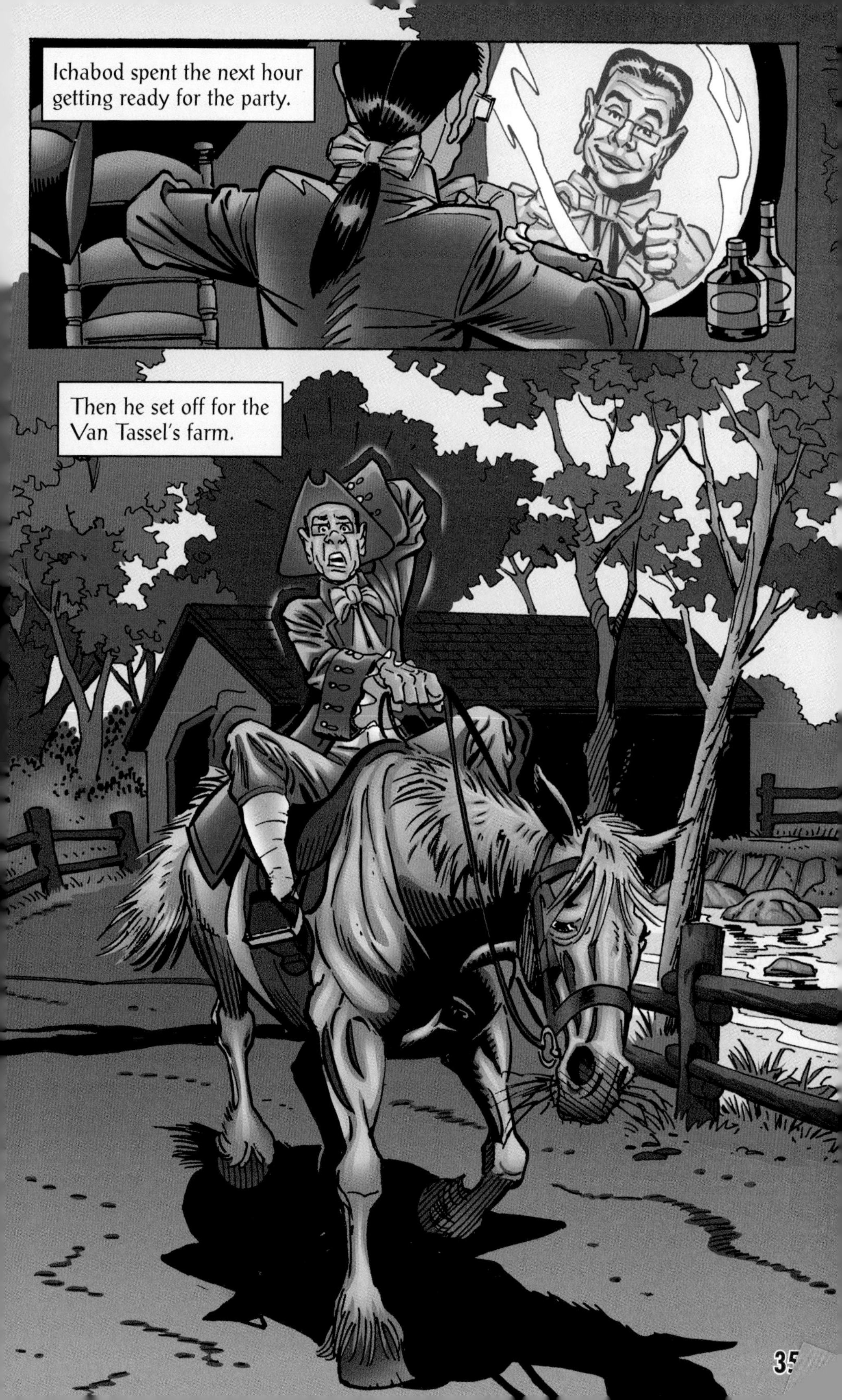
Ichabod spent the next hour getting ready for the party.
Then he set off for the Van Tassel's farm.

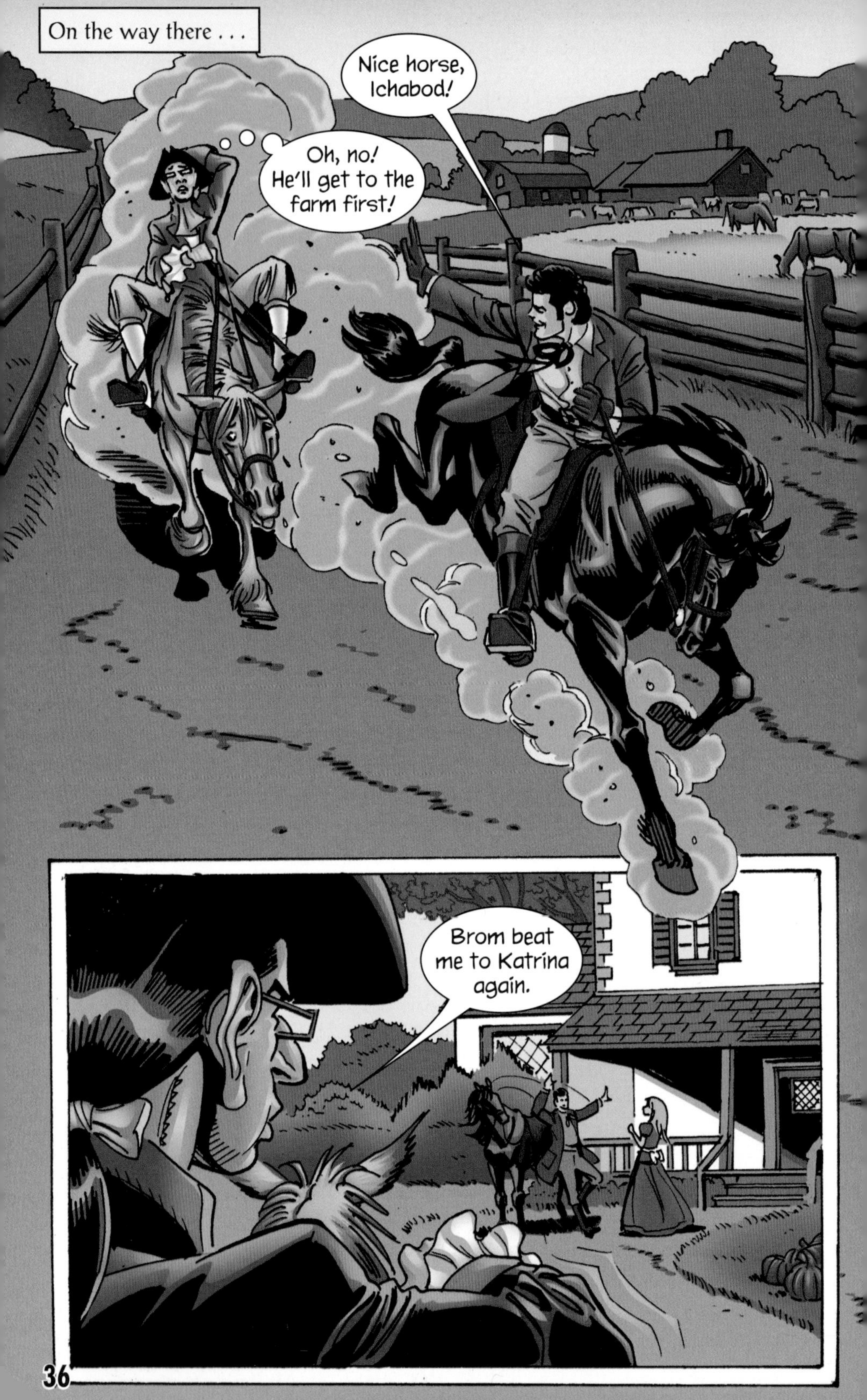
On the way there . . .
Nice horse, Ichabod!
Oh, no! He'll get to the farm first!
Brom beat me to Katrina again.

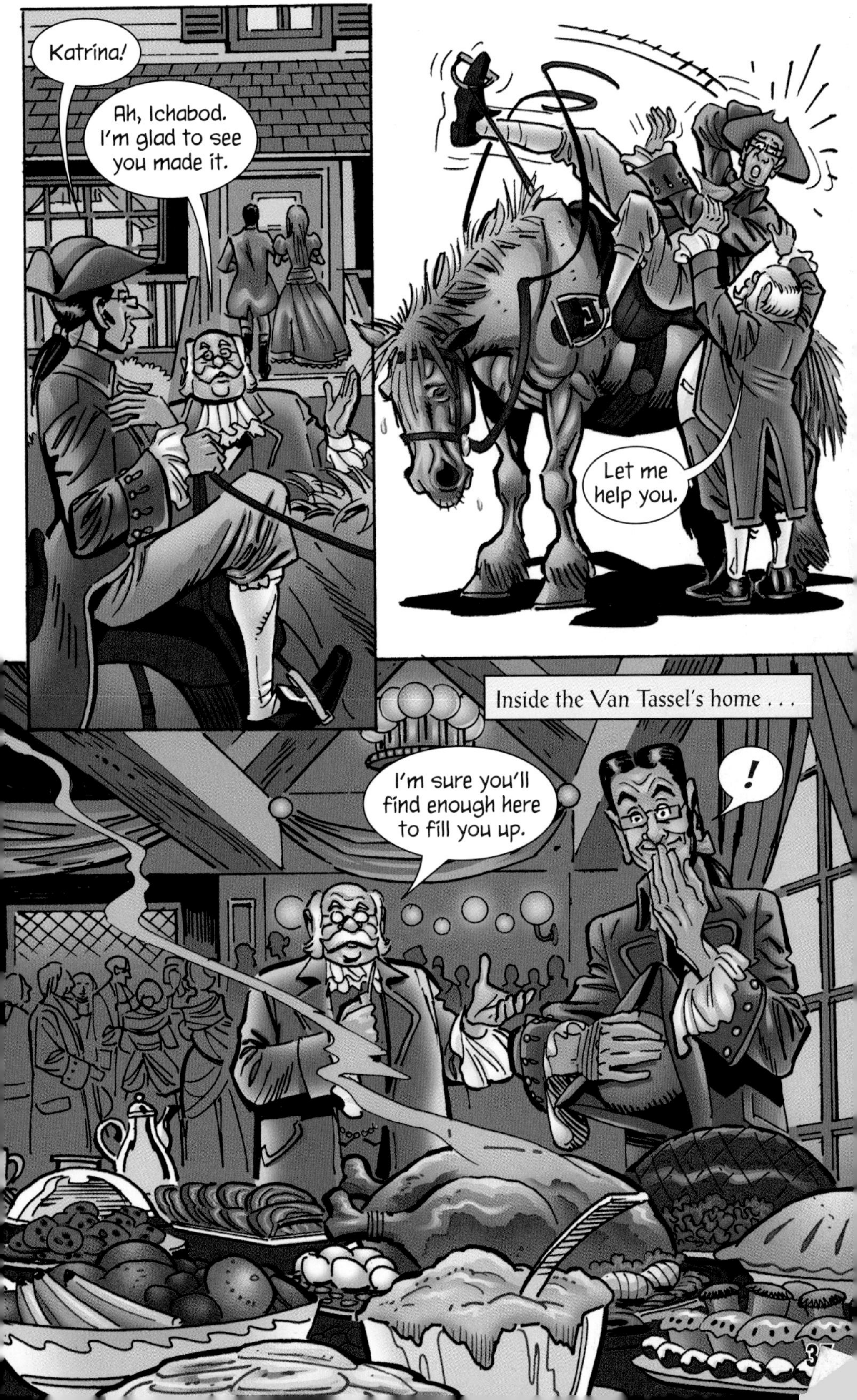
Katrina!
Ah, Ichabod. I'm glad to see you made it.
Let me help you.
Inside the Van Tassel's home . . .
I'm sure you'll find enough here to fill you up.
!

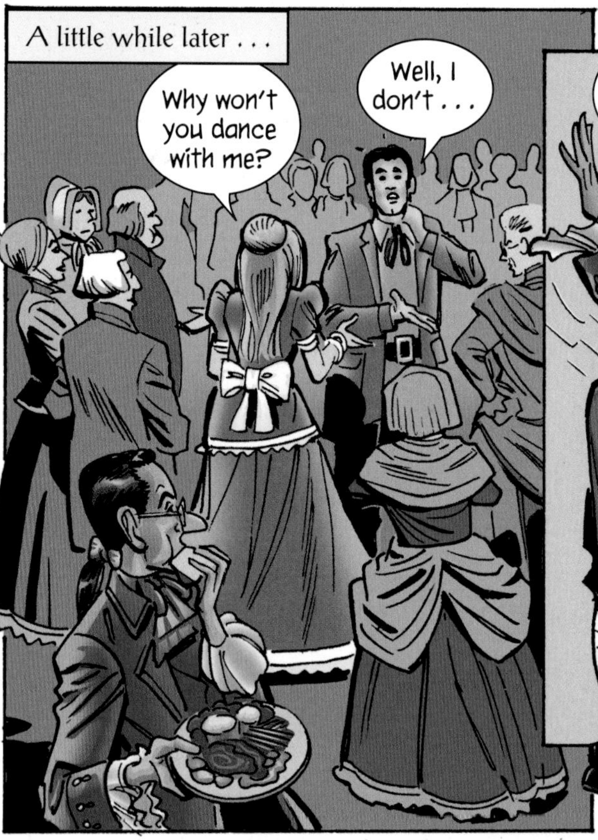
A little while later . . .
Why won't you dance with me?
Well, I don't . . .

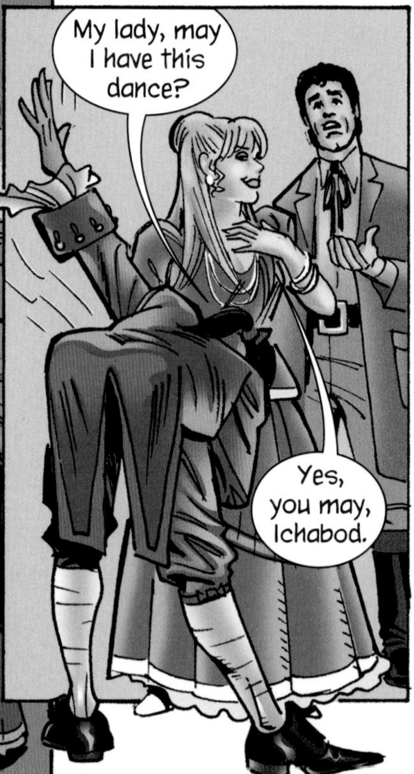
My lady, may I have this dance?
Yes, you may, Ichabod.

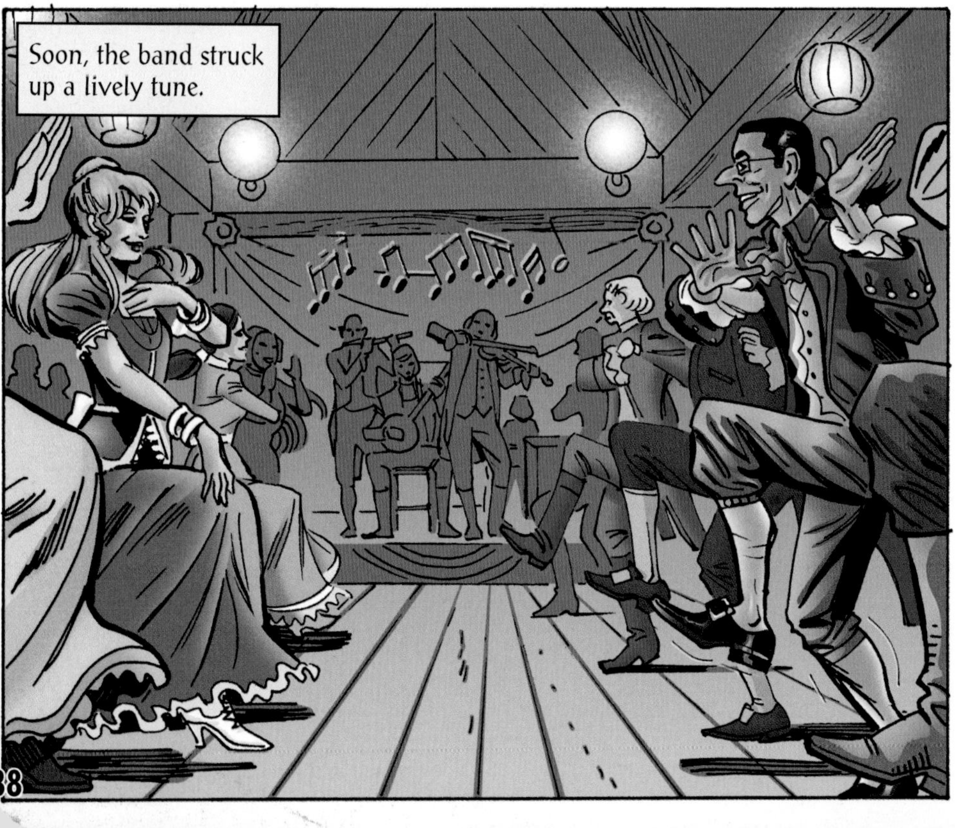
Soon, the band struck up a lively tune.

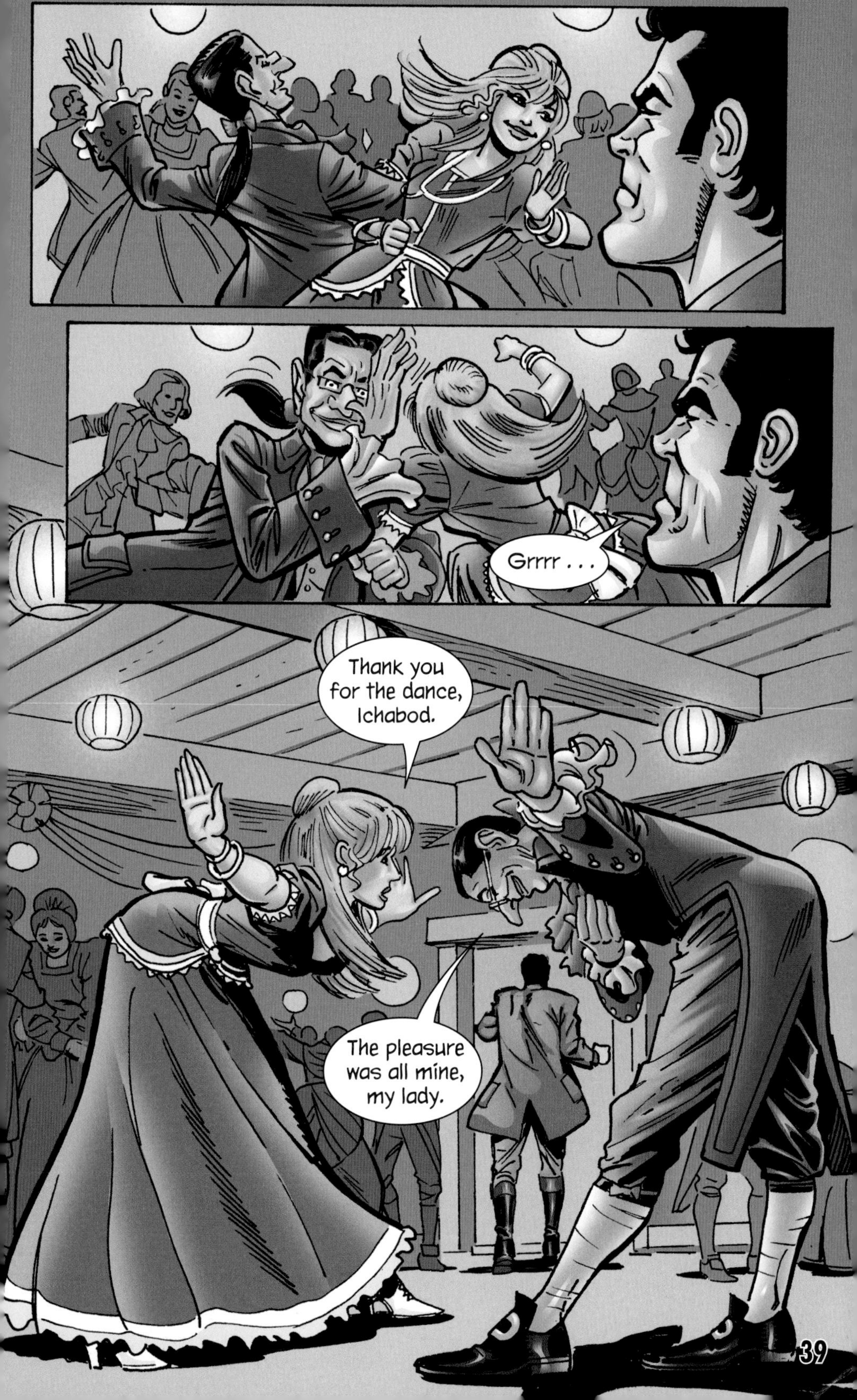

Grrrr . . .
Thank you for the dance, Ichabod.
The pleasure was all mine, my lady.

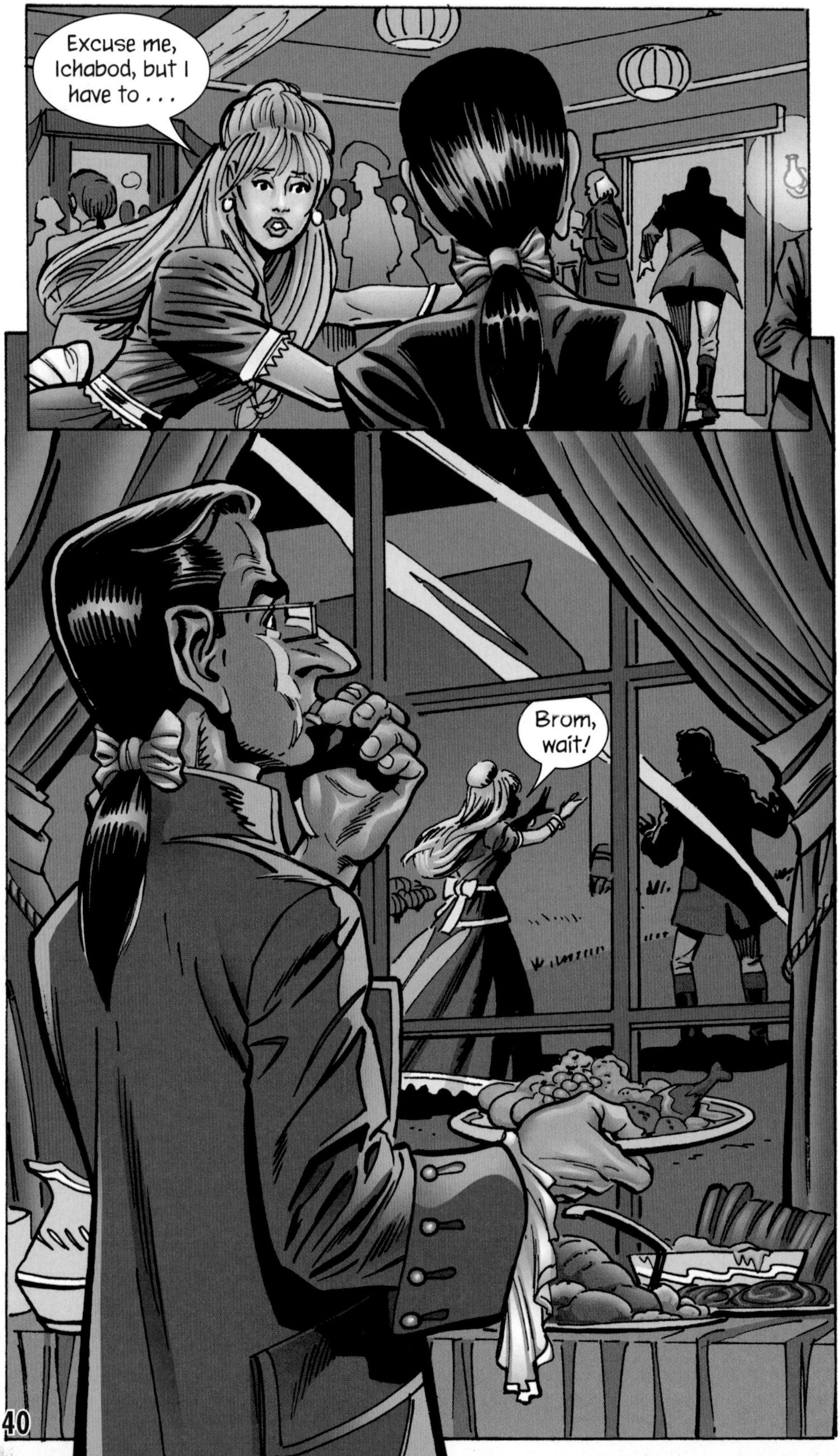
Excuse me, Ichabod, but I have to . . .
Brom, wait!

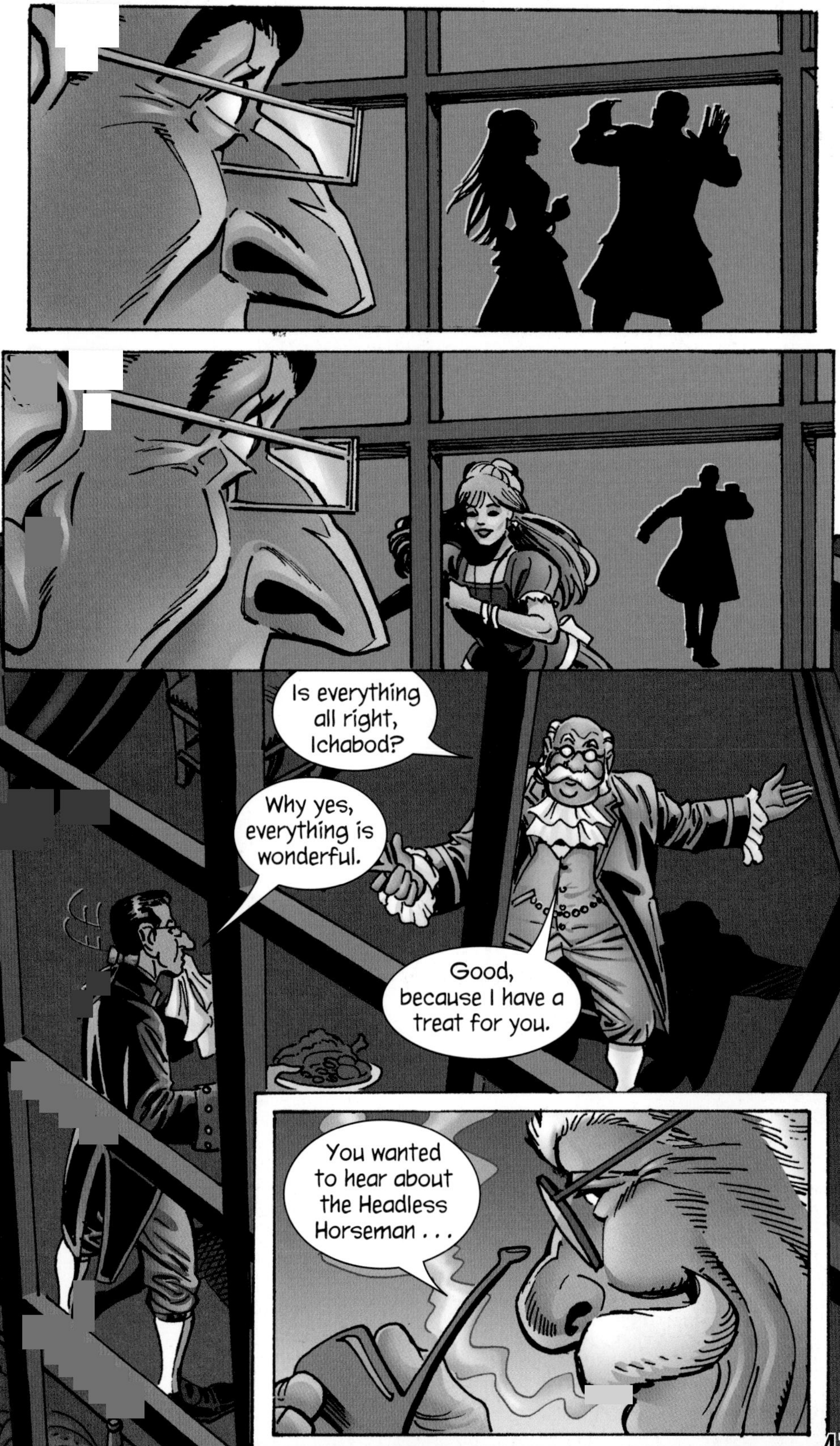

Is everything all right, Ichabod?
Why yes, everything is wonderful.
Good, because I have a treat for you.
You wanted to hear about the Headless Horseman . . .

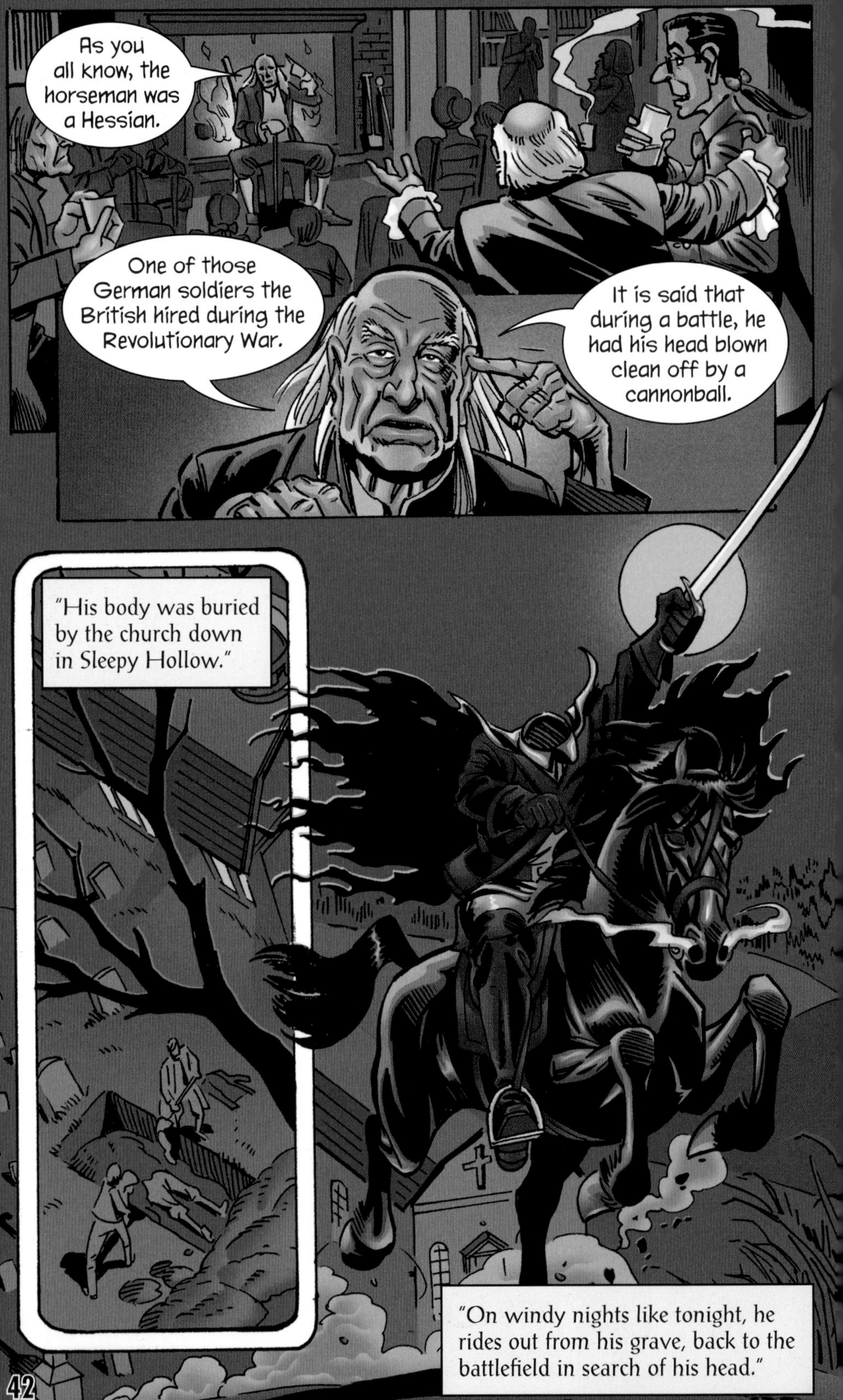
As you all know, the horseman was a Hessian.
One of those German soldiers the British hired during the Revolutionary War.
It is said that during a battle, he had his head blown clean off by a cannonball.
"His body was buried by the church down in Sleepy Hollow."
"On windy nights like tonight, he rides out from his grave, back to the battlefield in search of his head."

And don't forget what happened to old Brouwer . . .

"One night down in the Hollow, the Headless Horseman snatched him up and tossed old Brouwer on the back of his horse."

"Once they reached the bridge near the church, the Horseman turned into a skeleton."

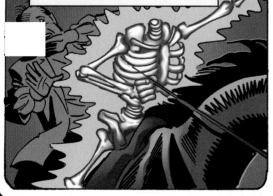

SPLASHH!

"He threw old Brouwer into the river and flew off over the trees."

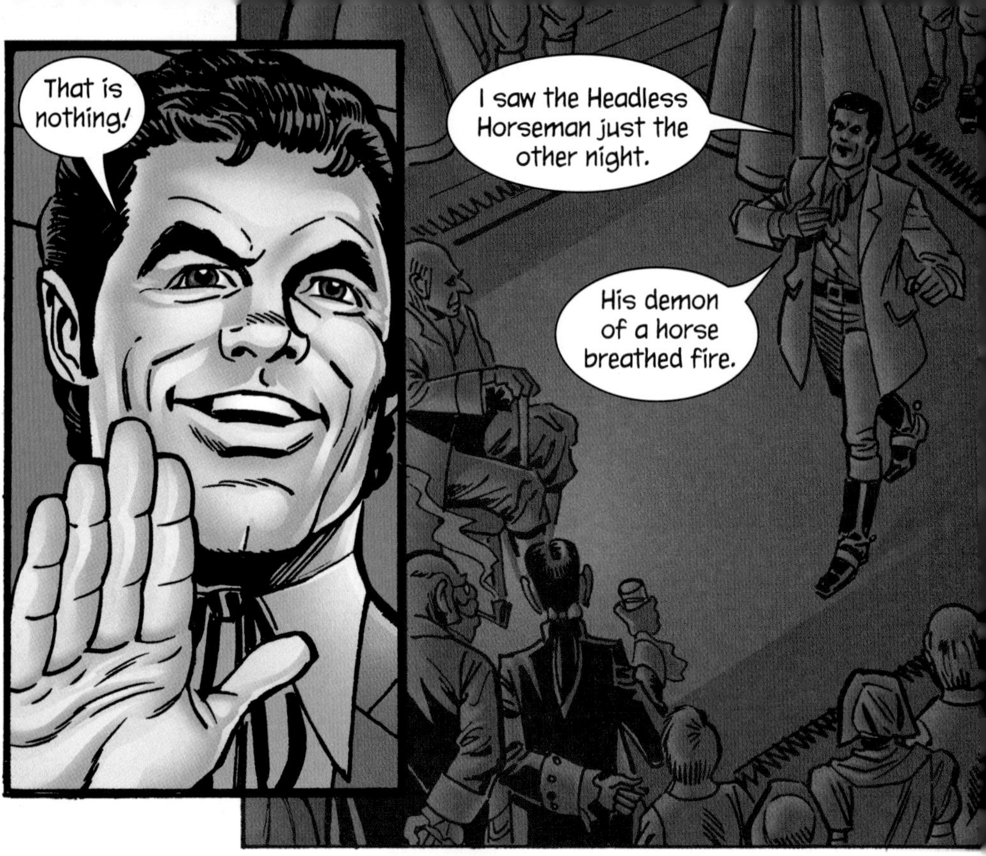
That is nothing!
I saw the Headless Horseman just the other night.
His demon of a horse breathed fire.

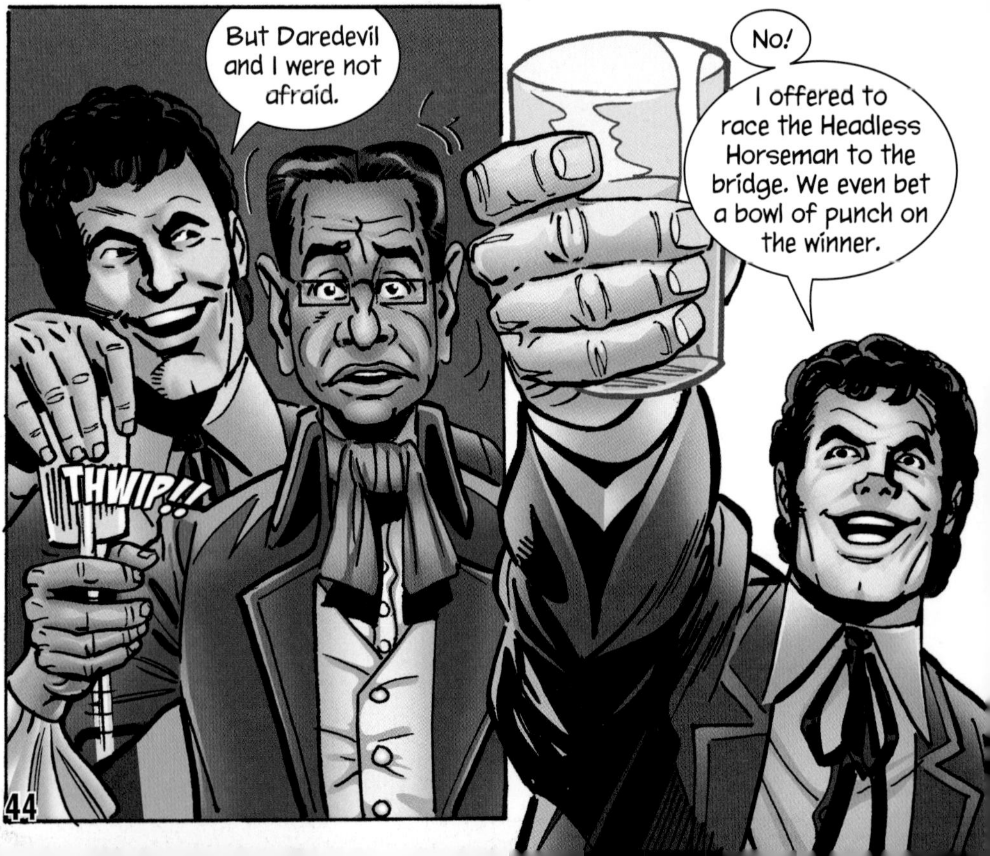
But Daredevil and I were not afraid.
No!
I offered to race the Headless Horseman to the bridge. We even bet a bowl of punch on the winner.
THWIP!!

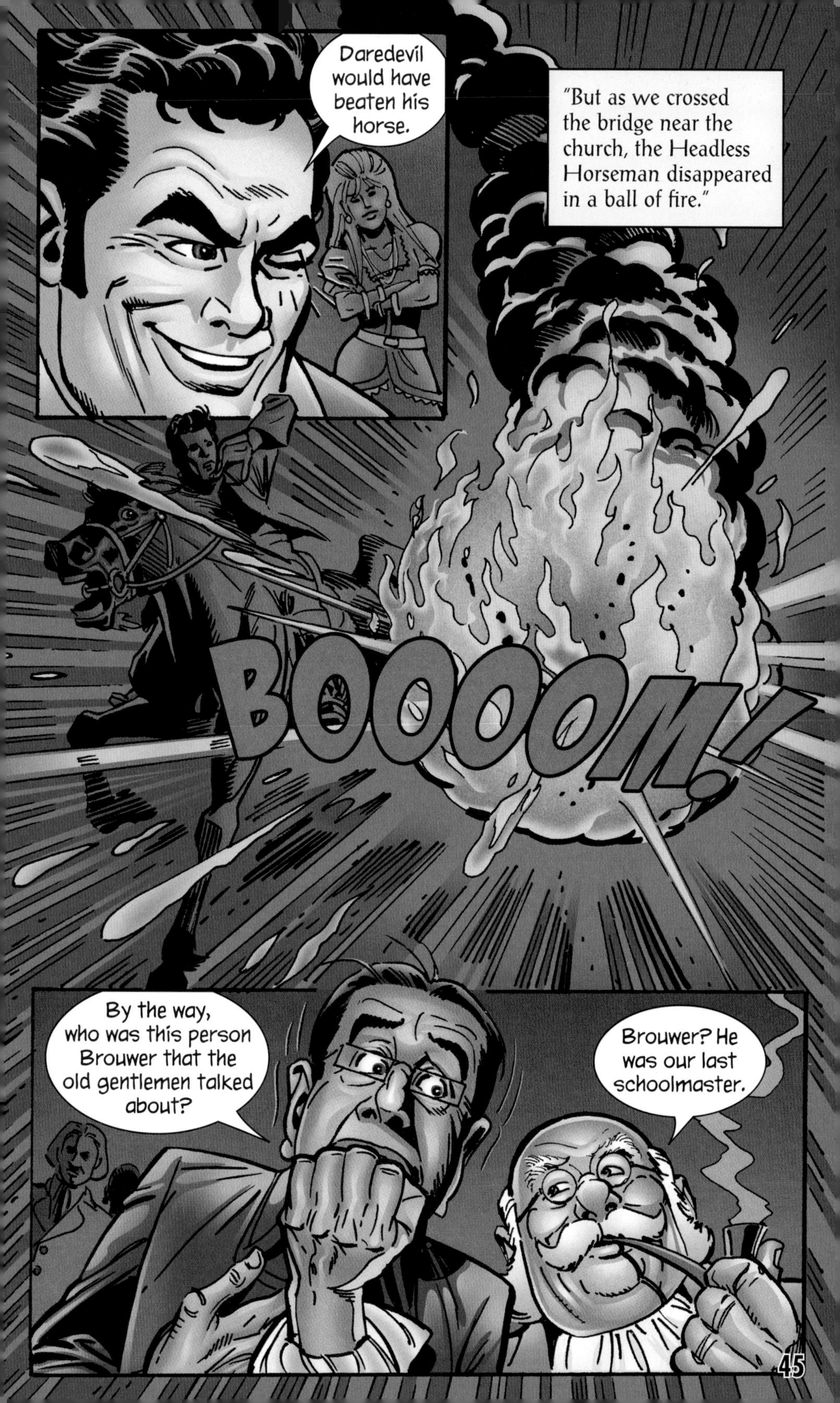
Daredevil would have beaten his horse.
"But as we crossed the bridge near the church, the Headless Horseman disappeared in a ball of fire."
BOOOOM!
By the way, who was this person Brouwer that the old gentlemen talked about?
Brouwer? He was our last schoolmaster.

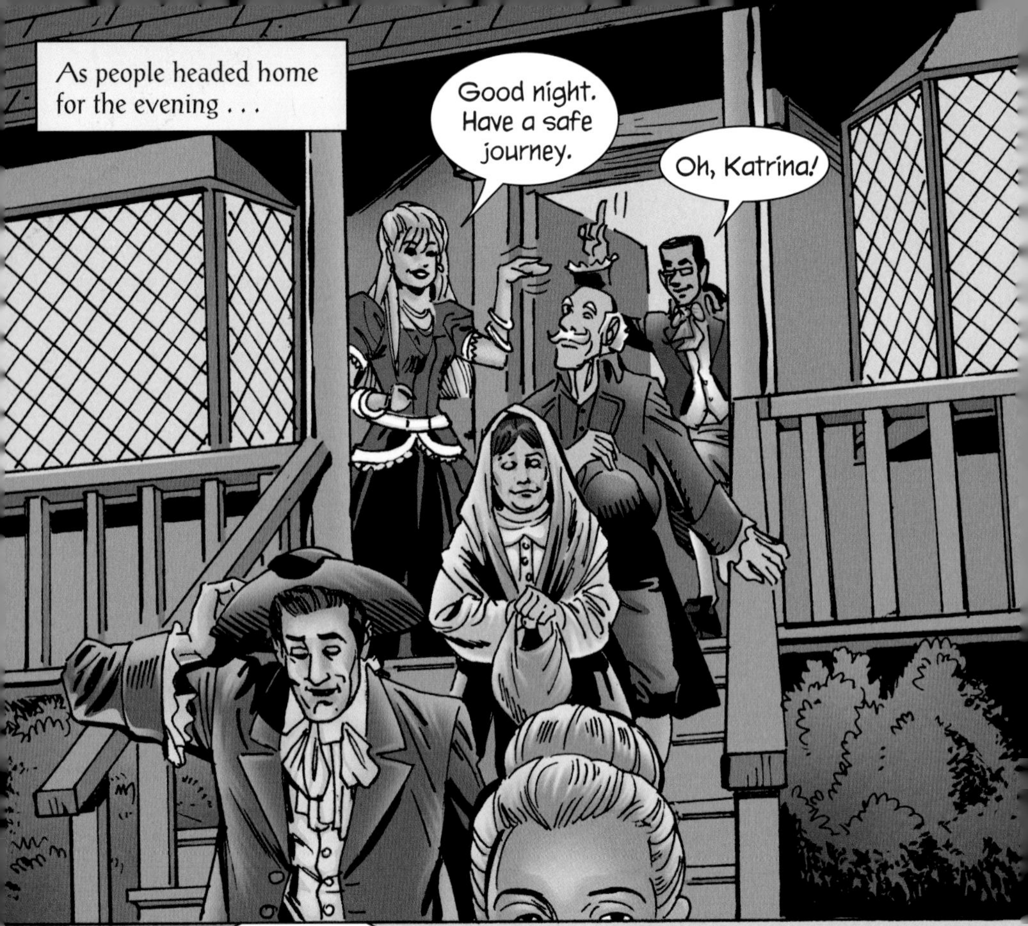
As people headed home for the evening . . .
Good night. Have a safe journey.
Oh, Katrina!

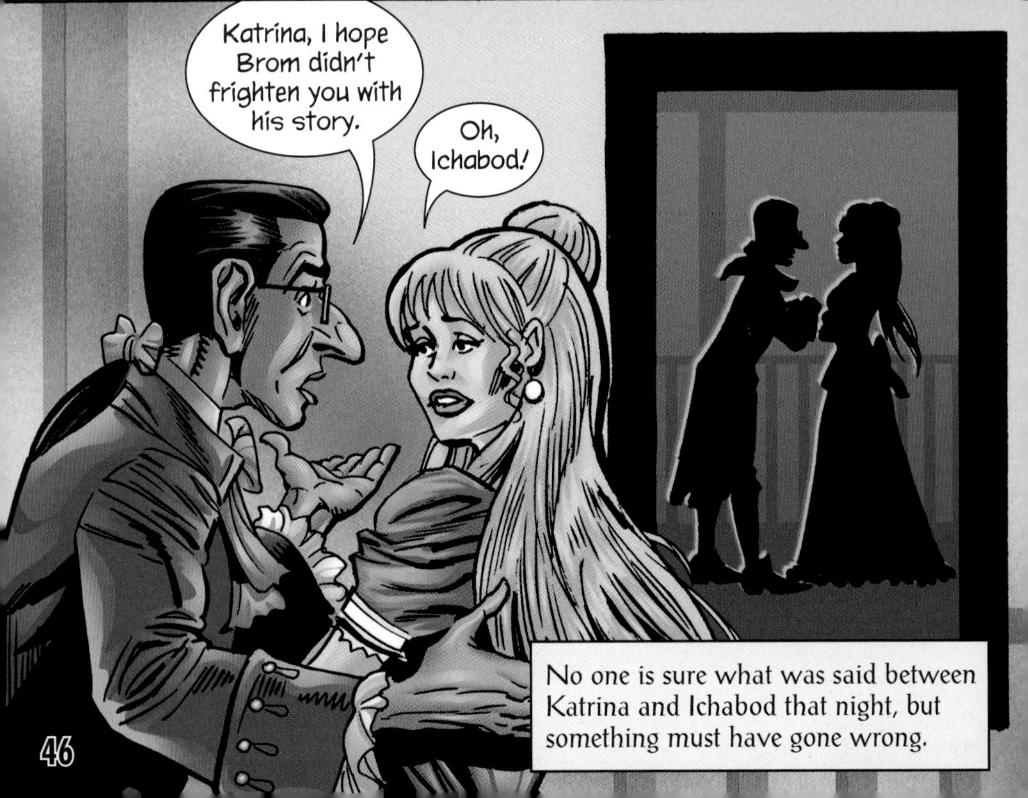
Katrina, I hope Brom didn't frighten you with his story.
Oh, Ichabod!
No one is sure what was said between Katrina and Ichabod that night, but something must have gone wrong.

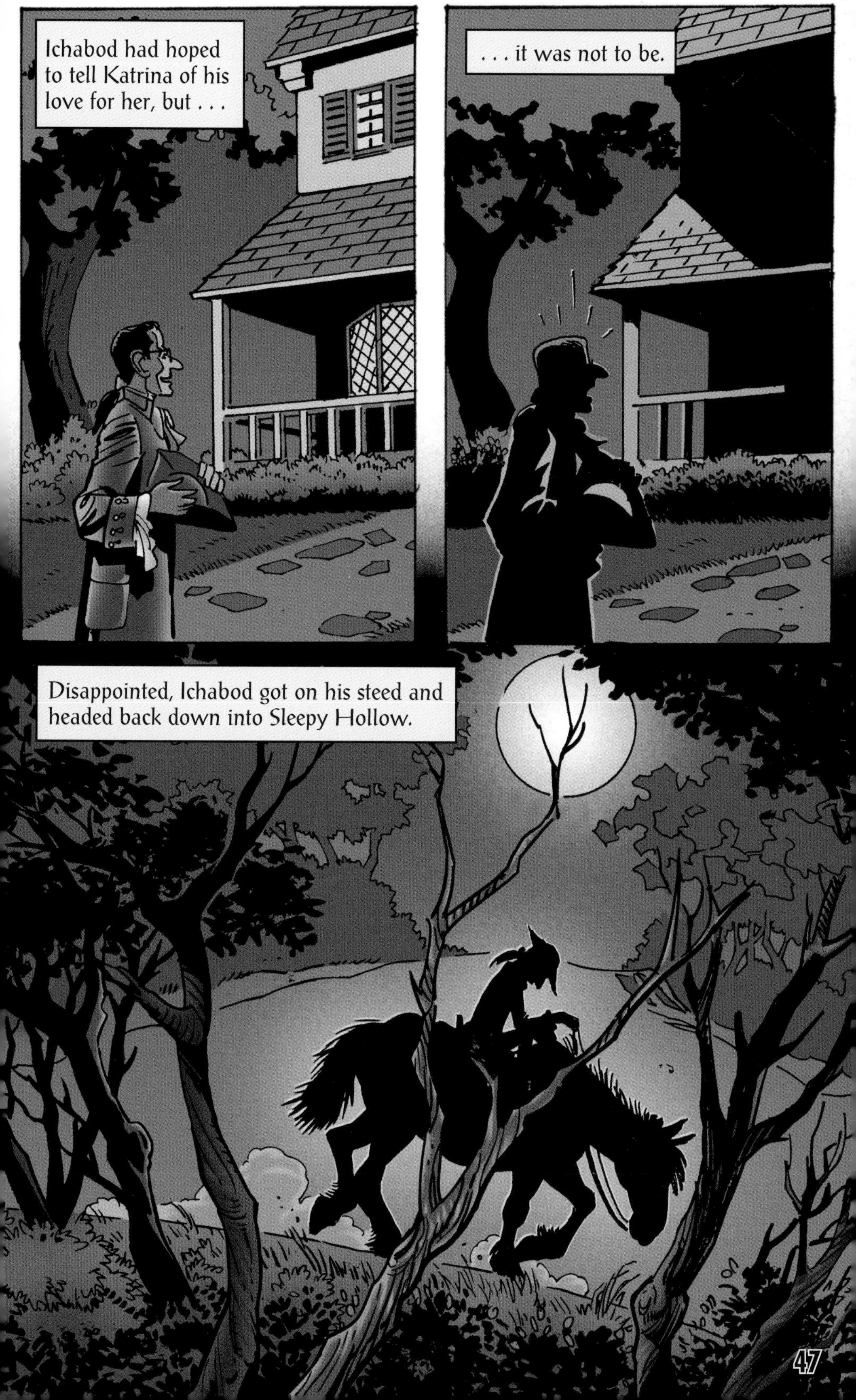
Ichabod had hoped to tell Katrina of his love for her, but . . .
. . . it was not to be.
Disappointed, Ichabod got on his steed and headed back down into Sleepy Hollow.

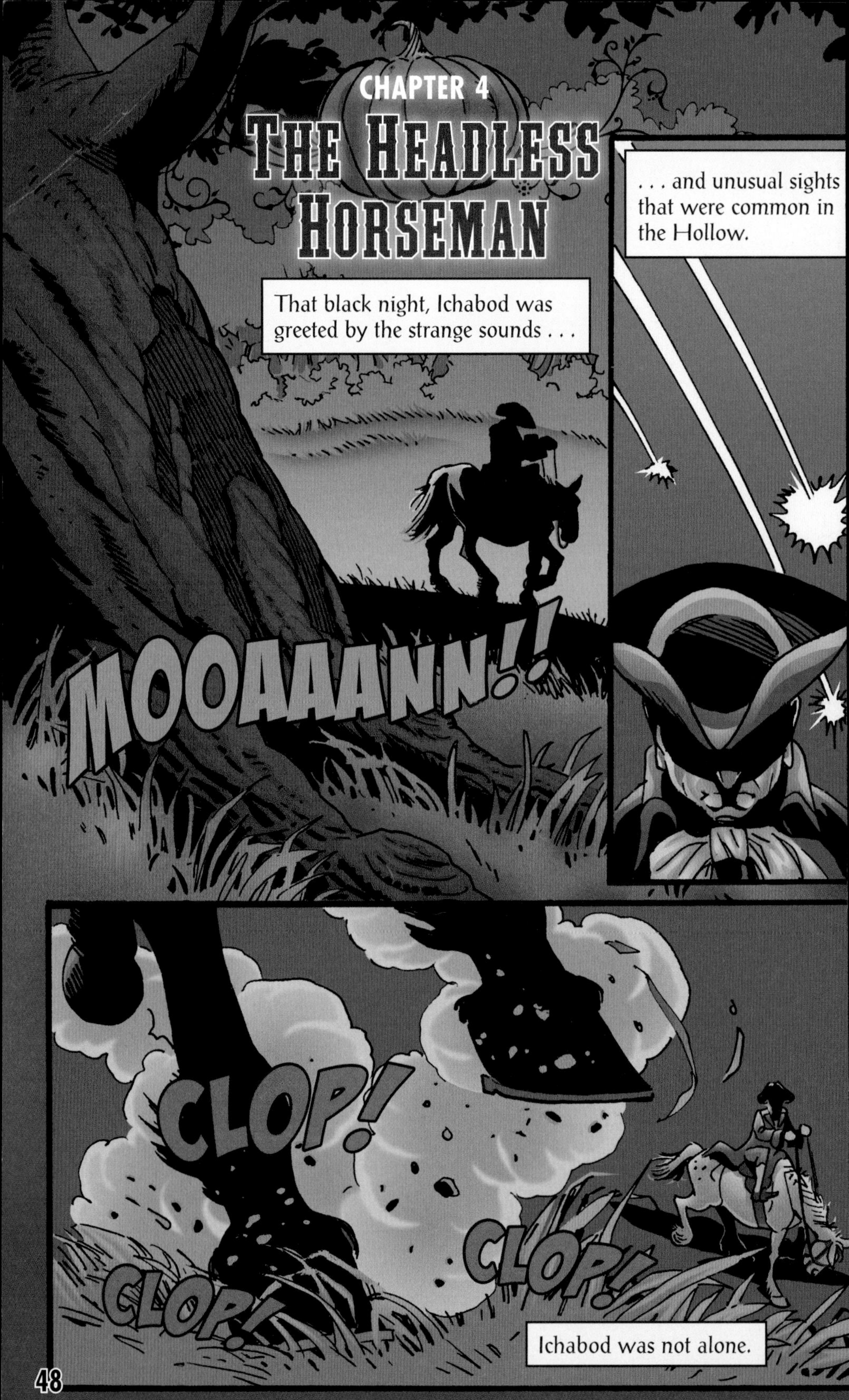

CHAPTER 4
THE HEADLESS HORSEMAN
That black night, Ichabod was greeted by the strange sounds . . .
. . . and unusual sights that were common in the Hollow.
MOOAAAANN!!
CLOP!
CLOP!
CLOP!
Ichabod was not alone.

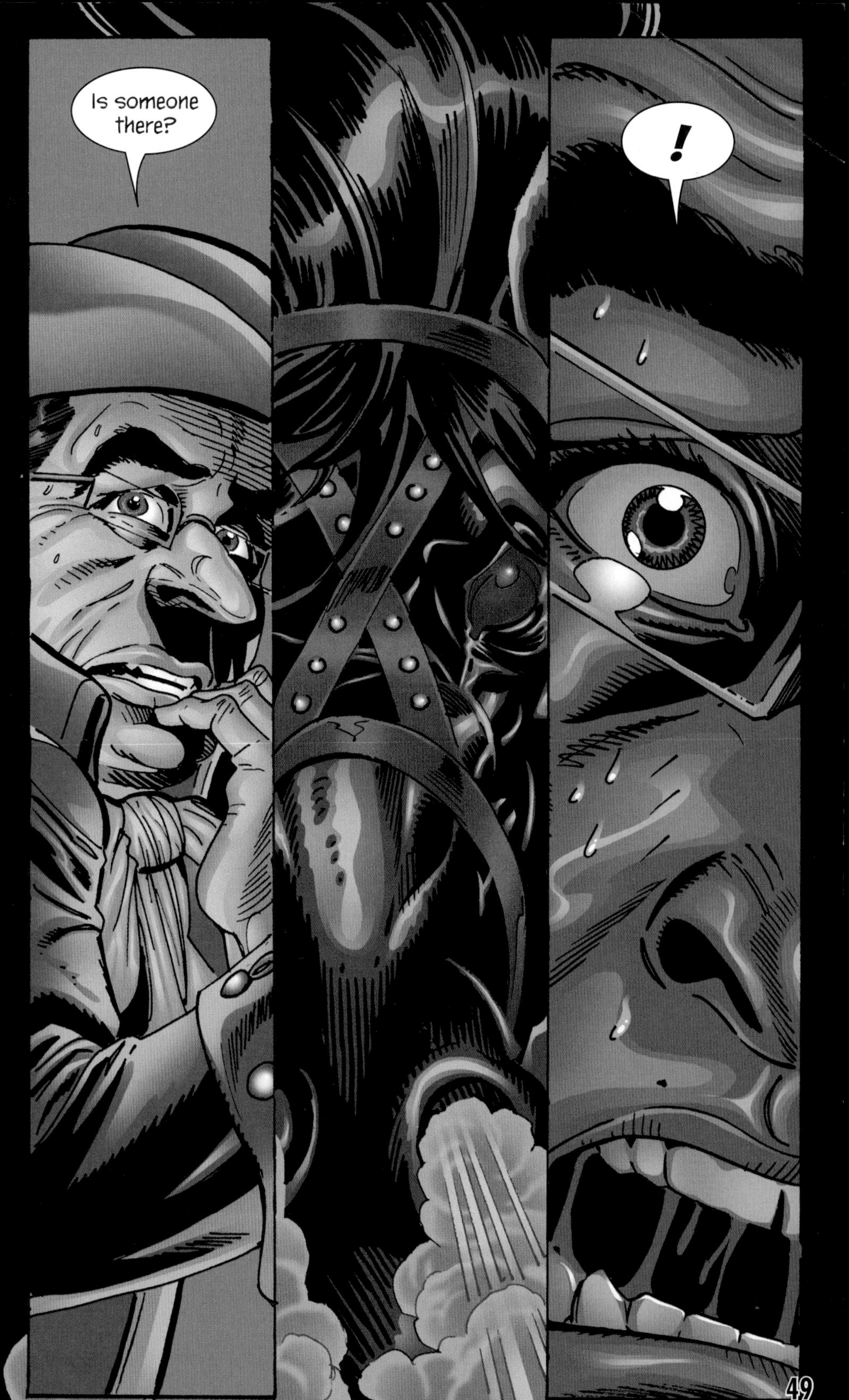
Is someone there?
!

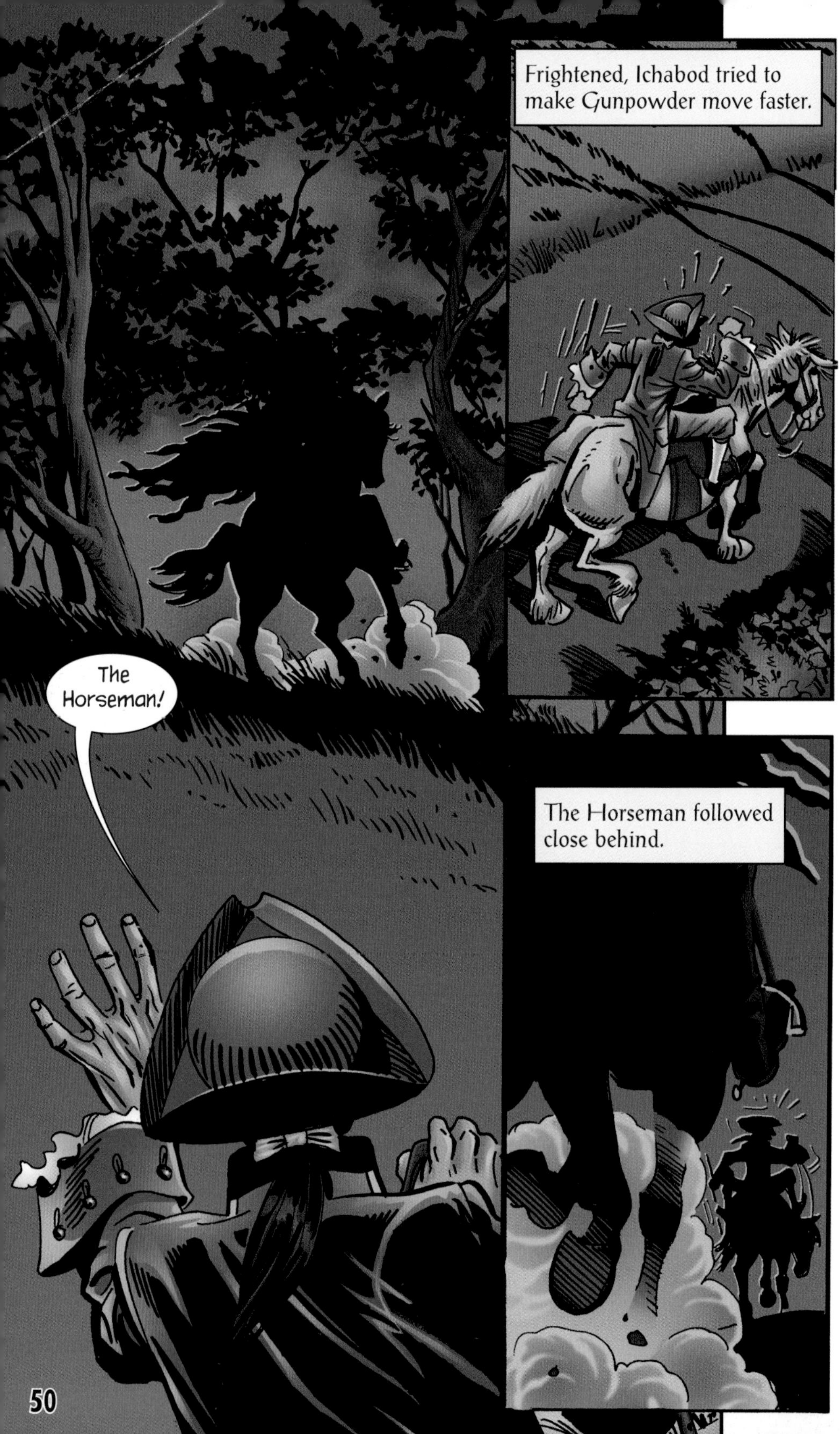
Frightened, Ichabod tried to make Gunpowder move faster.
The Horseman!
The Horseman followed close behind.

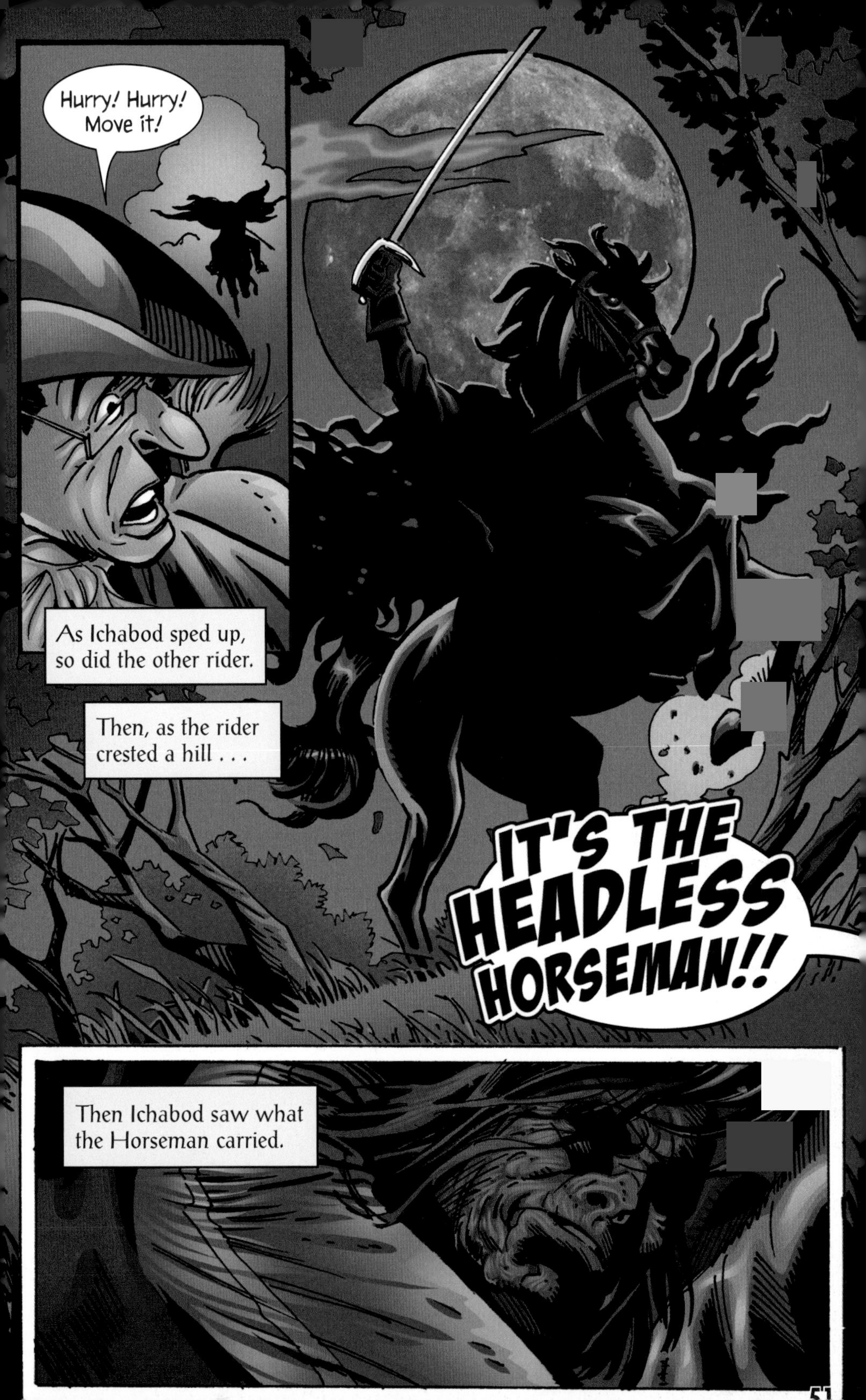
Hurry! Hurry! Move it!
As Ichabod sped up, so did the other rider.
Then, as the rider crested a hill . . .
IT'S THE HEADLESS HORSEMAN!!
Then Ichabod saw what the Horseman carried.

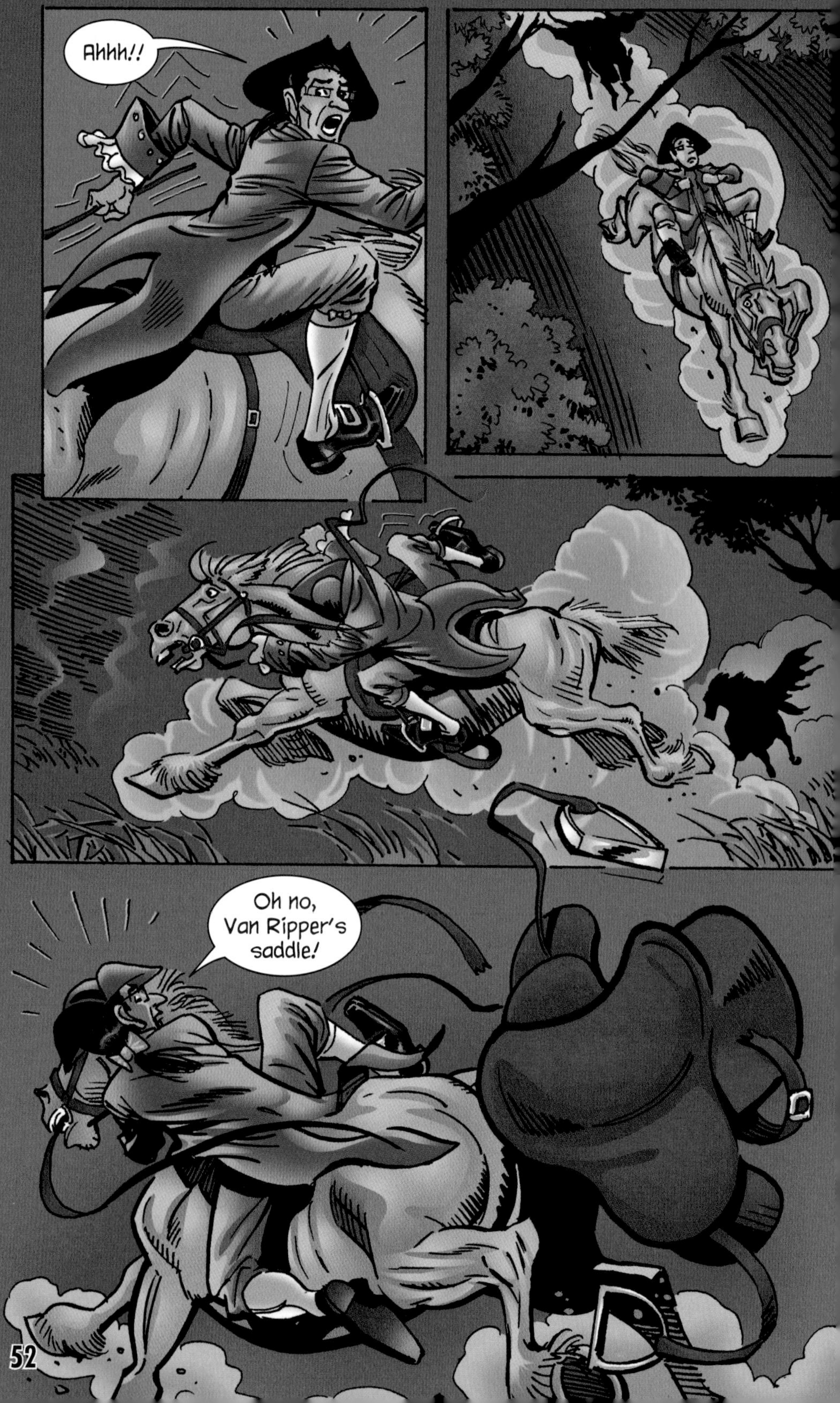
Ahhh!!
Oh no, Van Ripper's saddle!

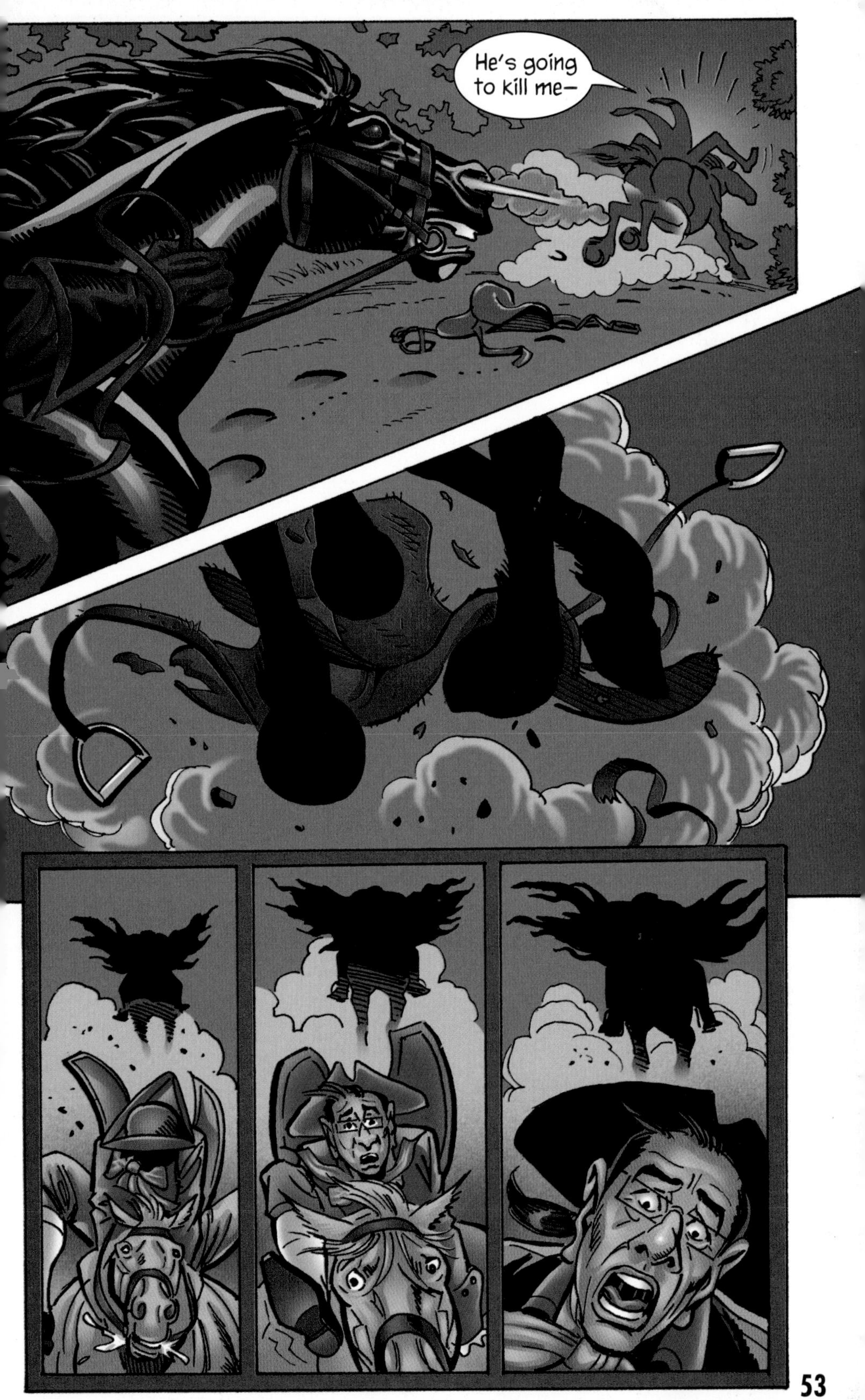
He's going to kill me—

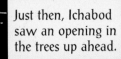

Just then, Ichabod saw an opening in the trees up ahead.

He saw the bridge where Brom said the Headless Horseman had disappeared.

If I can only reach that bridge.

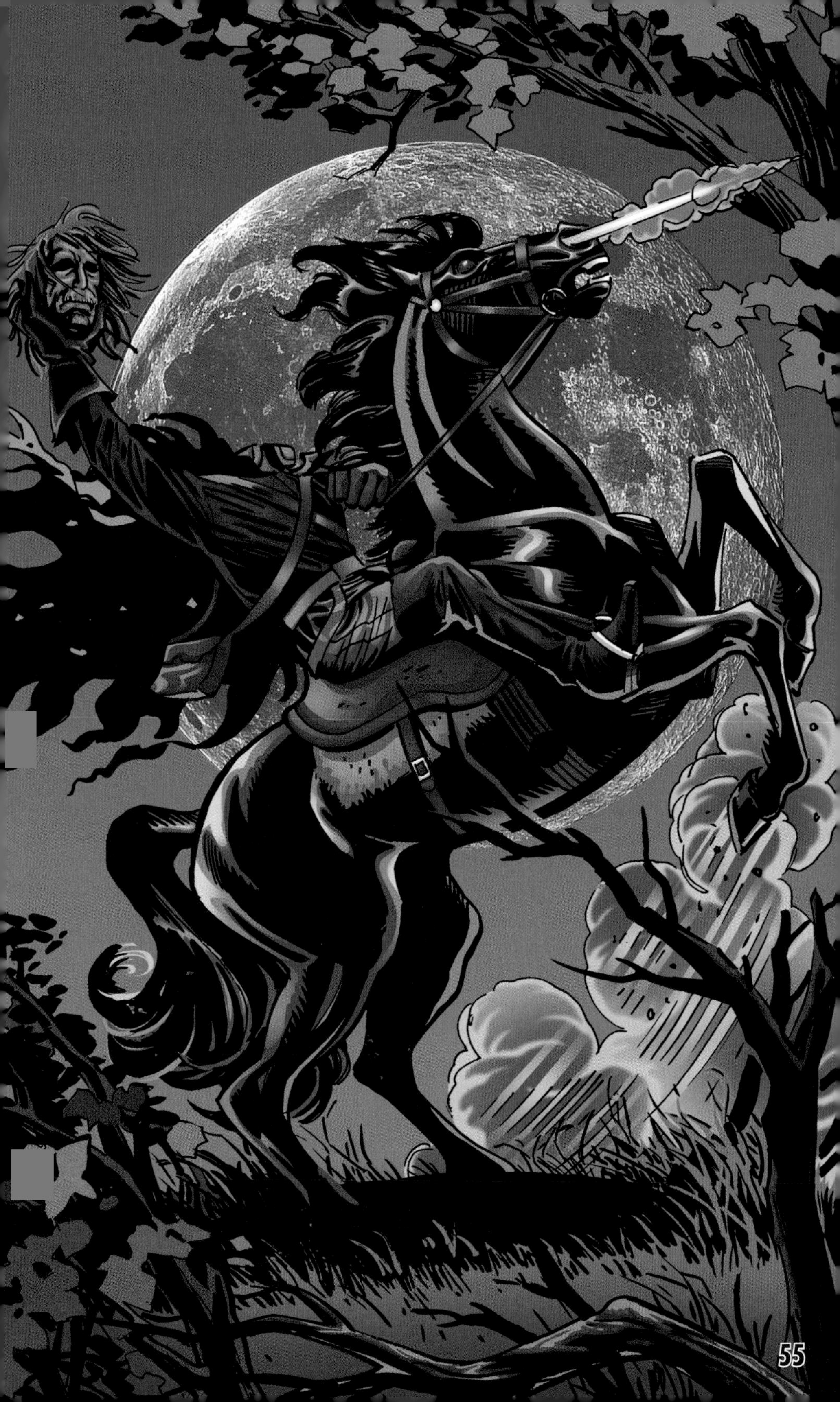

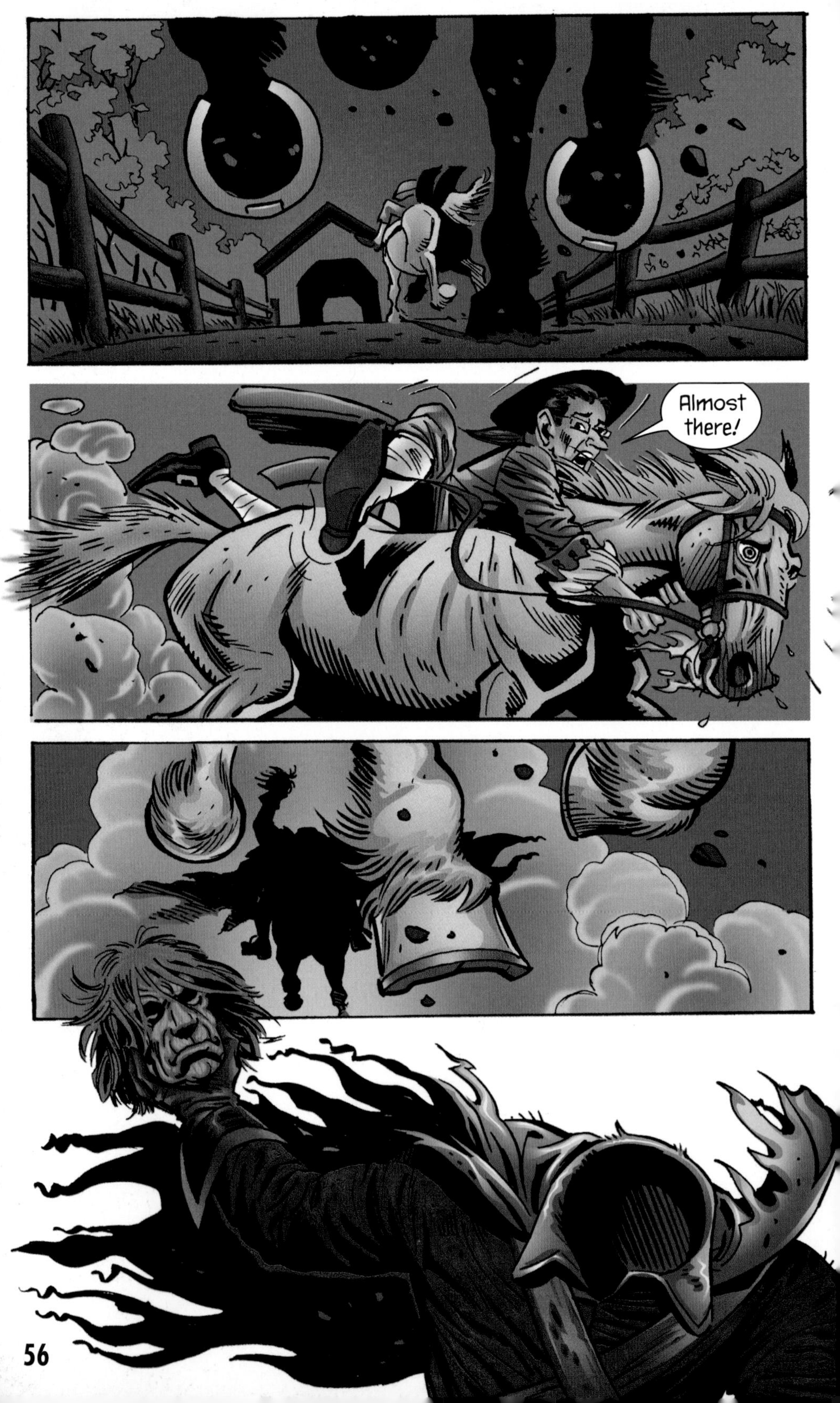
Almost
there!

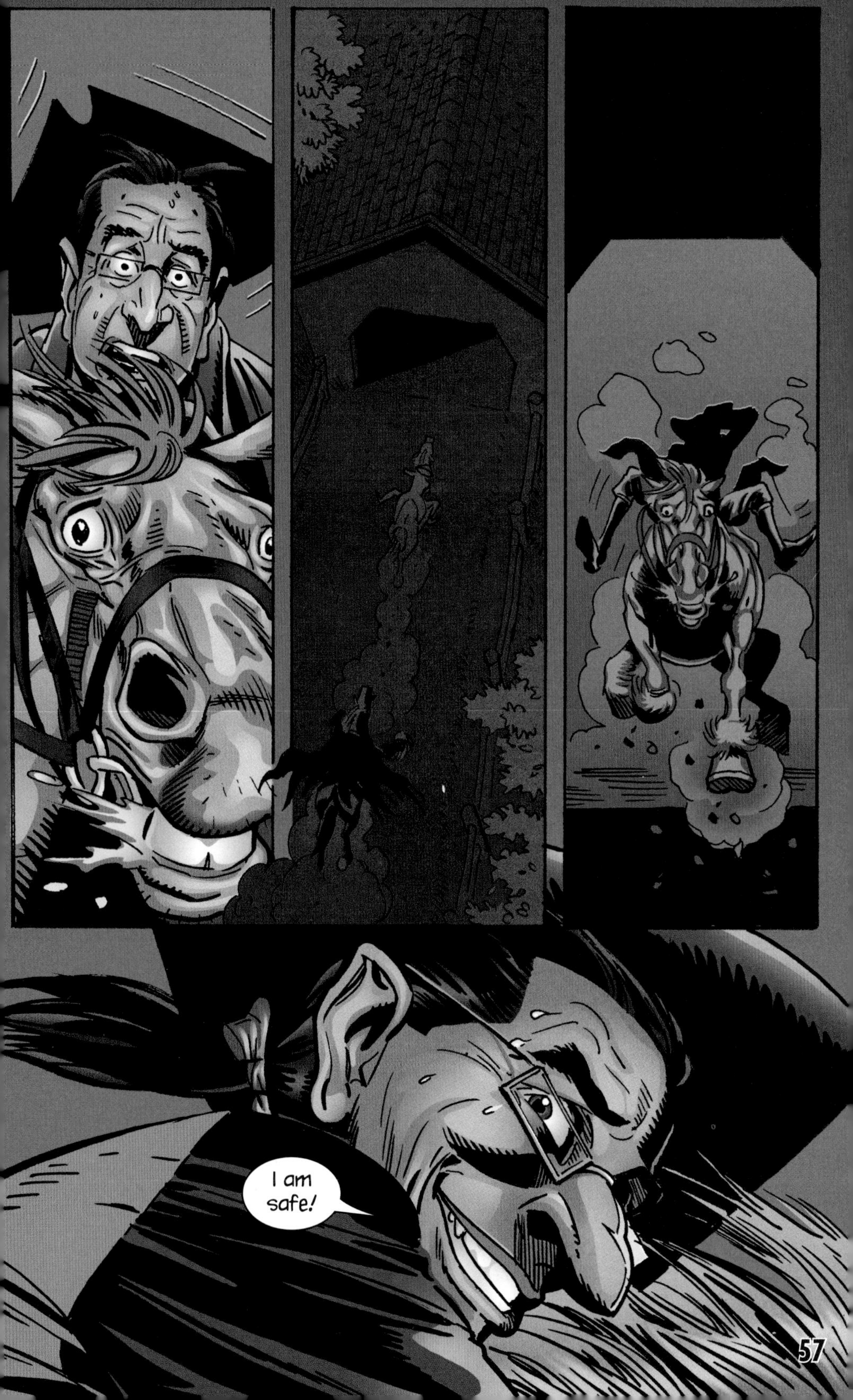
I am safe!

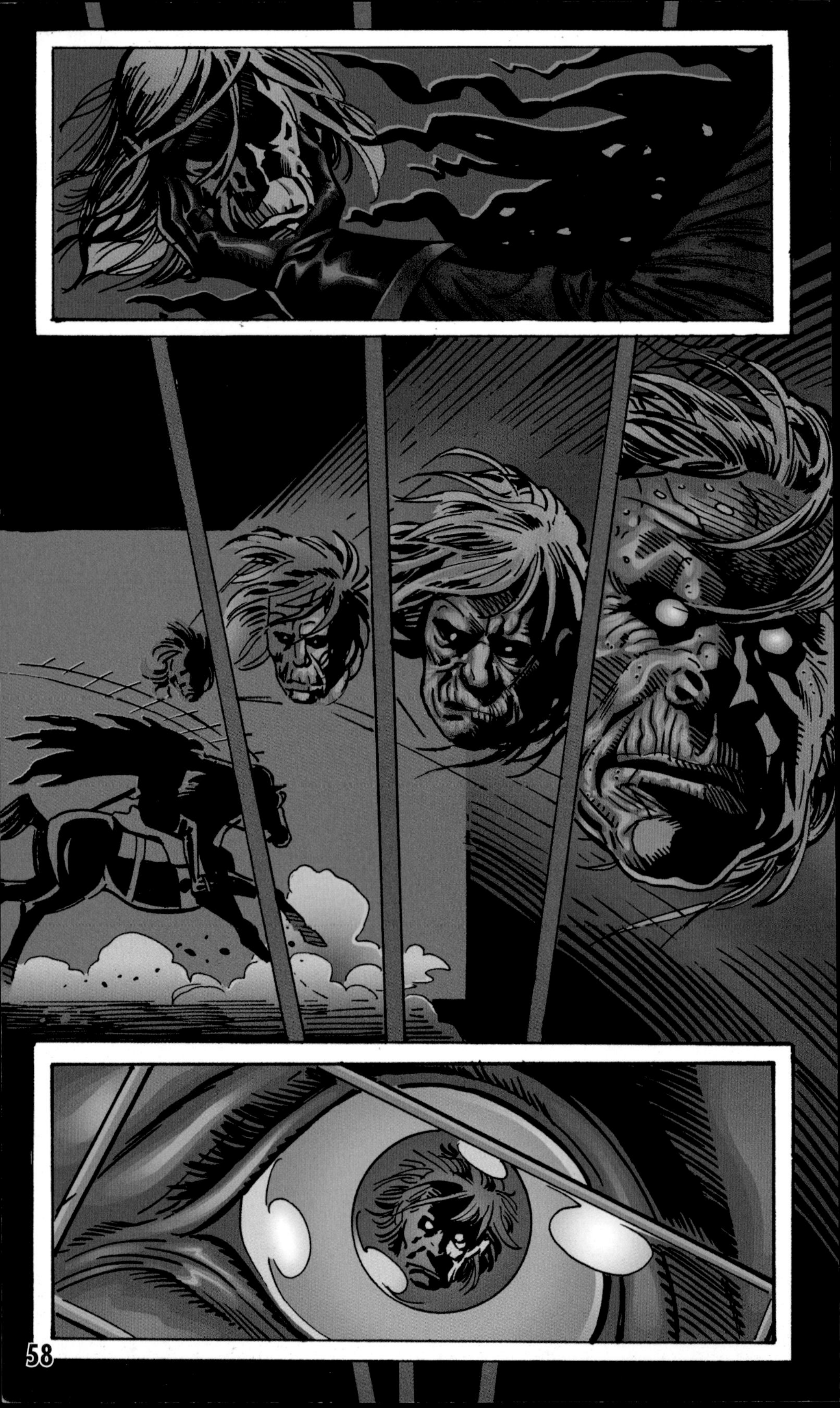

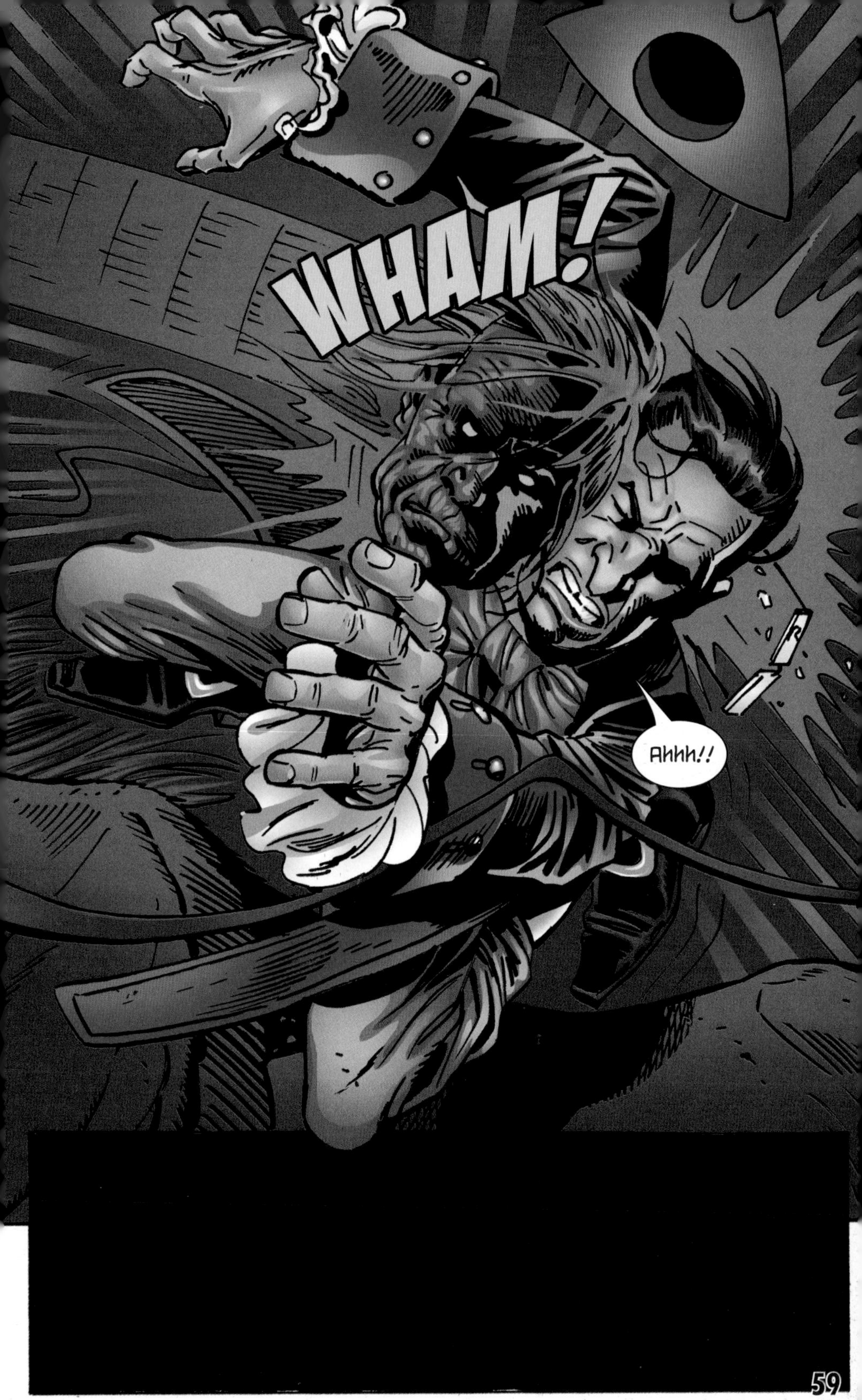
WHAM!
Ahhh!!

[redacted]

CHAPTER 5
THE NEW LEGEND

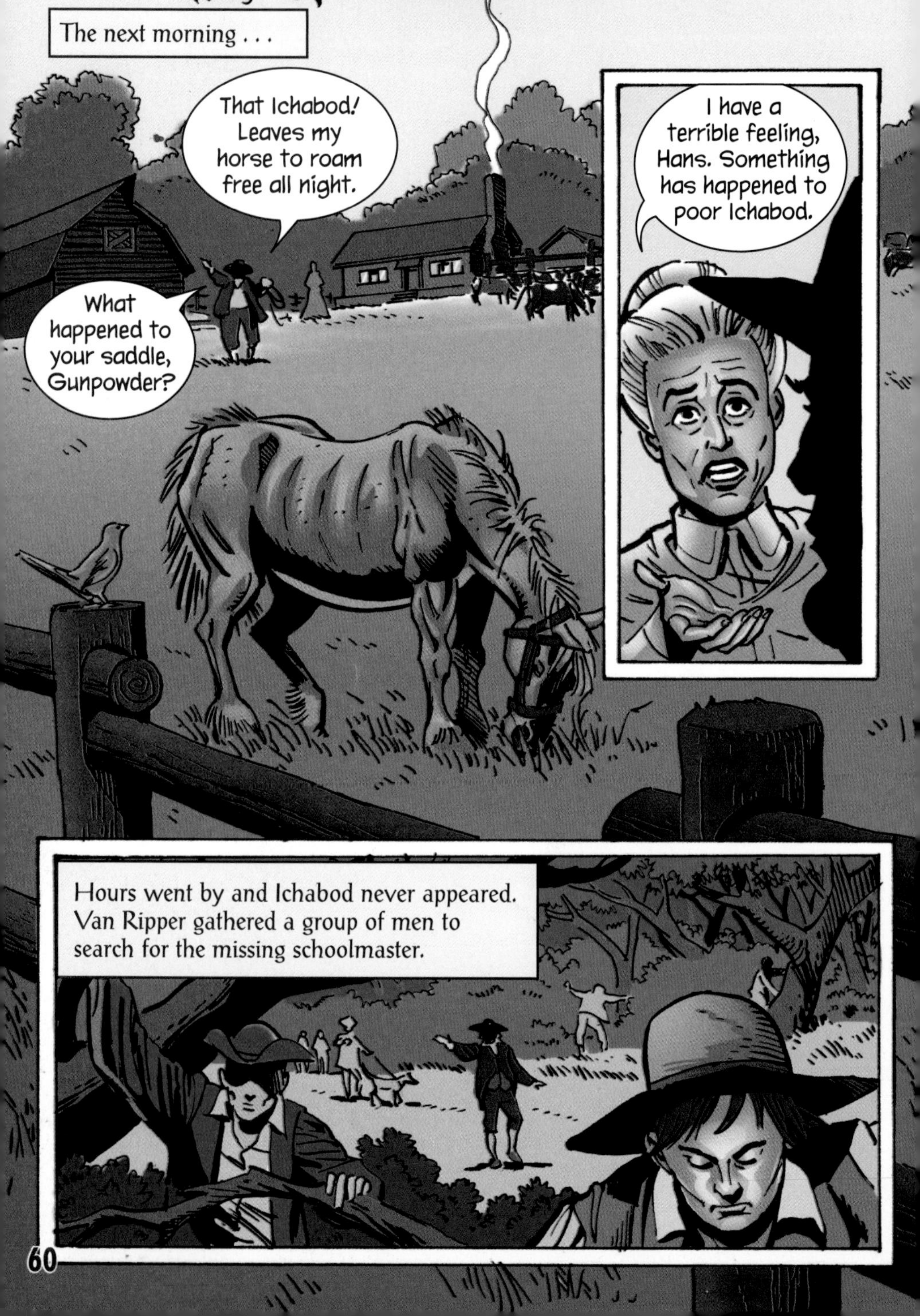

The next morning . . .
What happened to your saddle, Gunpowder?
That Ichabod! Leaves my horse to roam free all night.
I have a terrible feeling, Hans. Something has happened to poor Ichabod.
Hours went by and Ichabod never appeared. Van Ripper gathered a group of men to search for the missing schoolmaster.

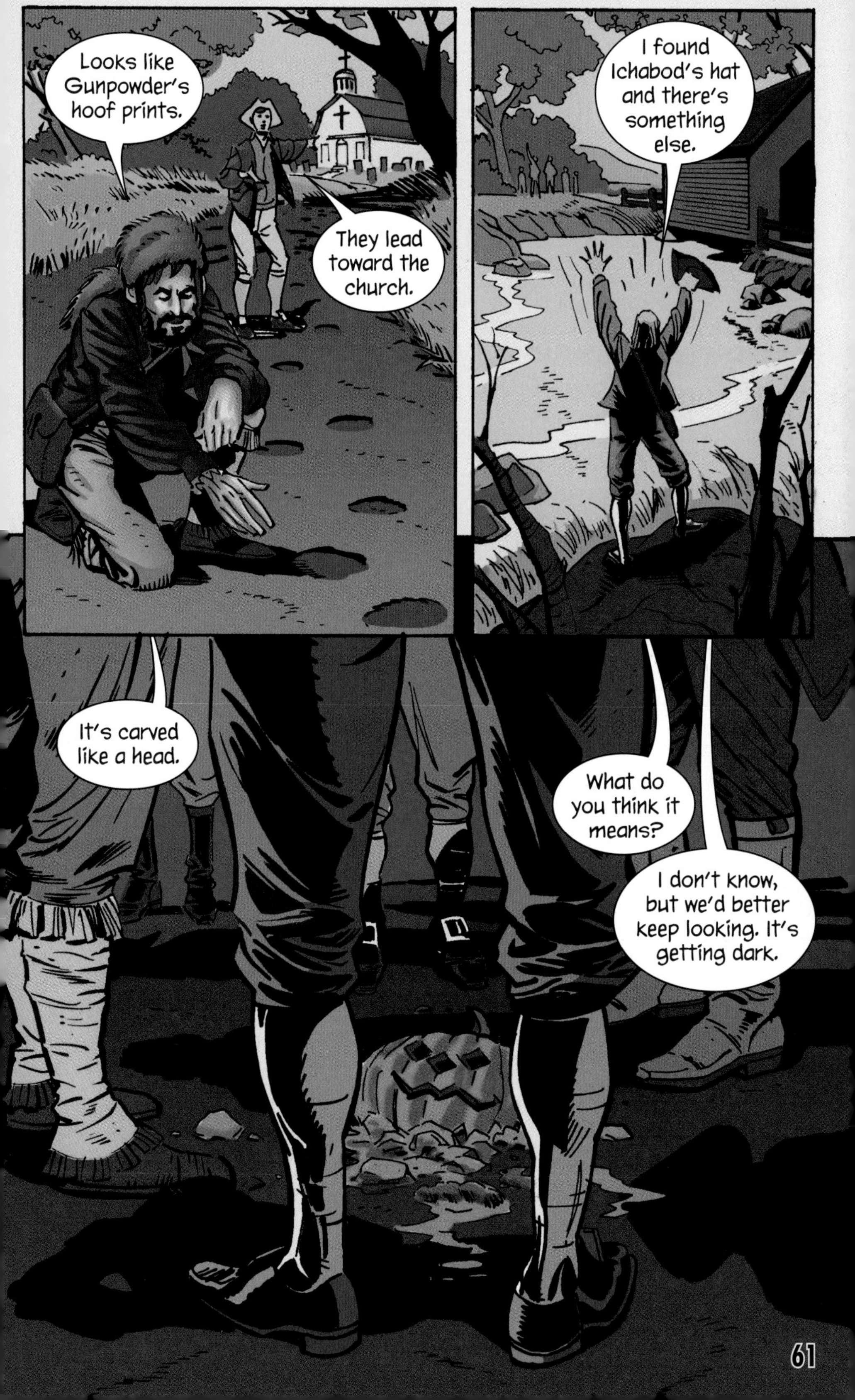

Looks like Gunpowder's hoof prints.
They lead toward the church.
I found Ichabod's hat and there's something else.
It's carved like a head.
What do you think it means?
I don't know, but we'd better keep looking. It's getting dark.

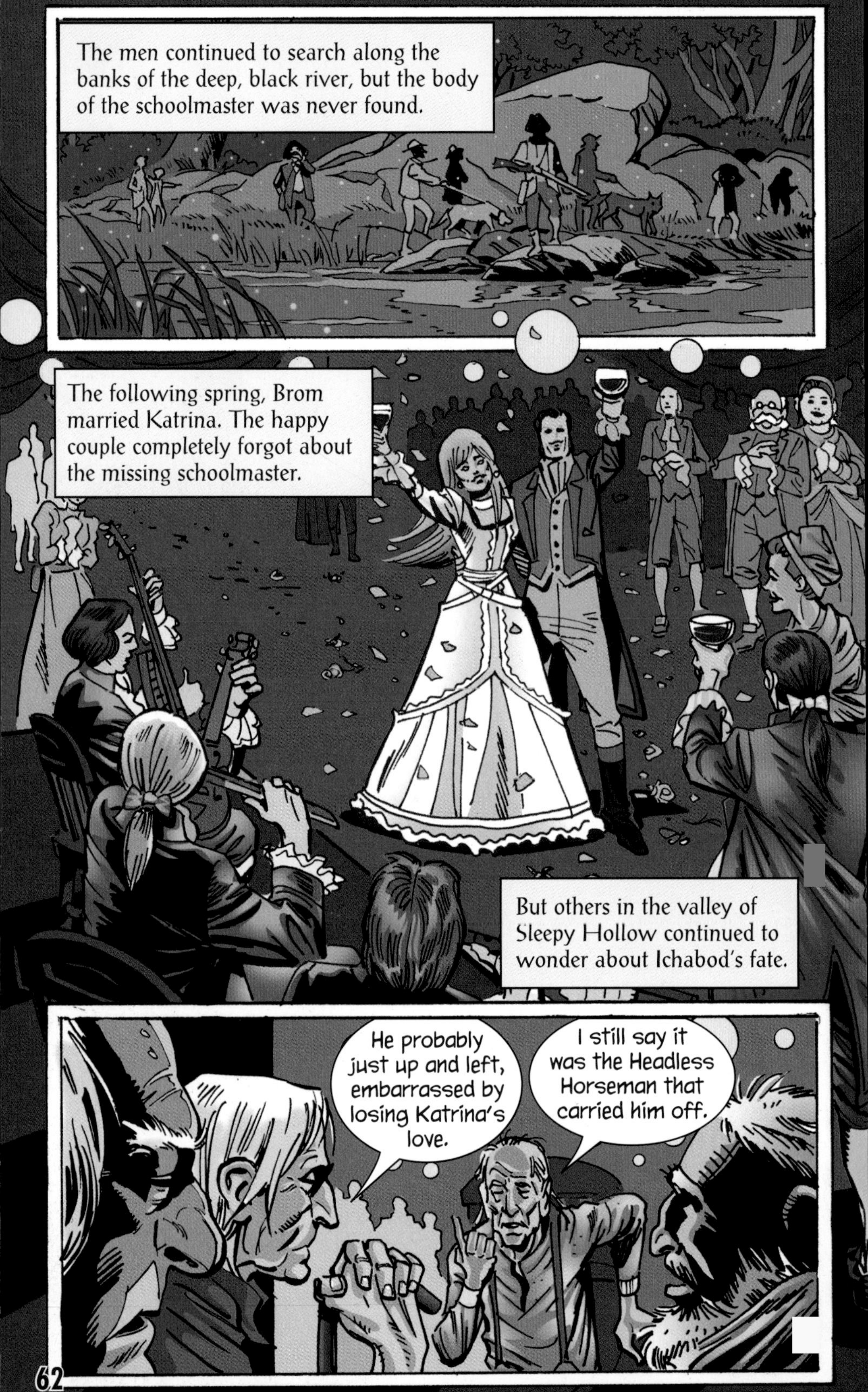

The men continued to search along the banks of the deep, black river, but the body of the schoolmaster was never found.
The following spring, Brom married Katrina. The happy couple completely forgot about the missing schoolmaster.
But others in the valley of Sleepy Hollow continued to wonder about Ichabod's fate.
He probably just up and left, embarrassed by losing Katrina's love.
I still say it was the Headless Horseman that carried him off.

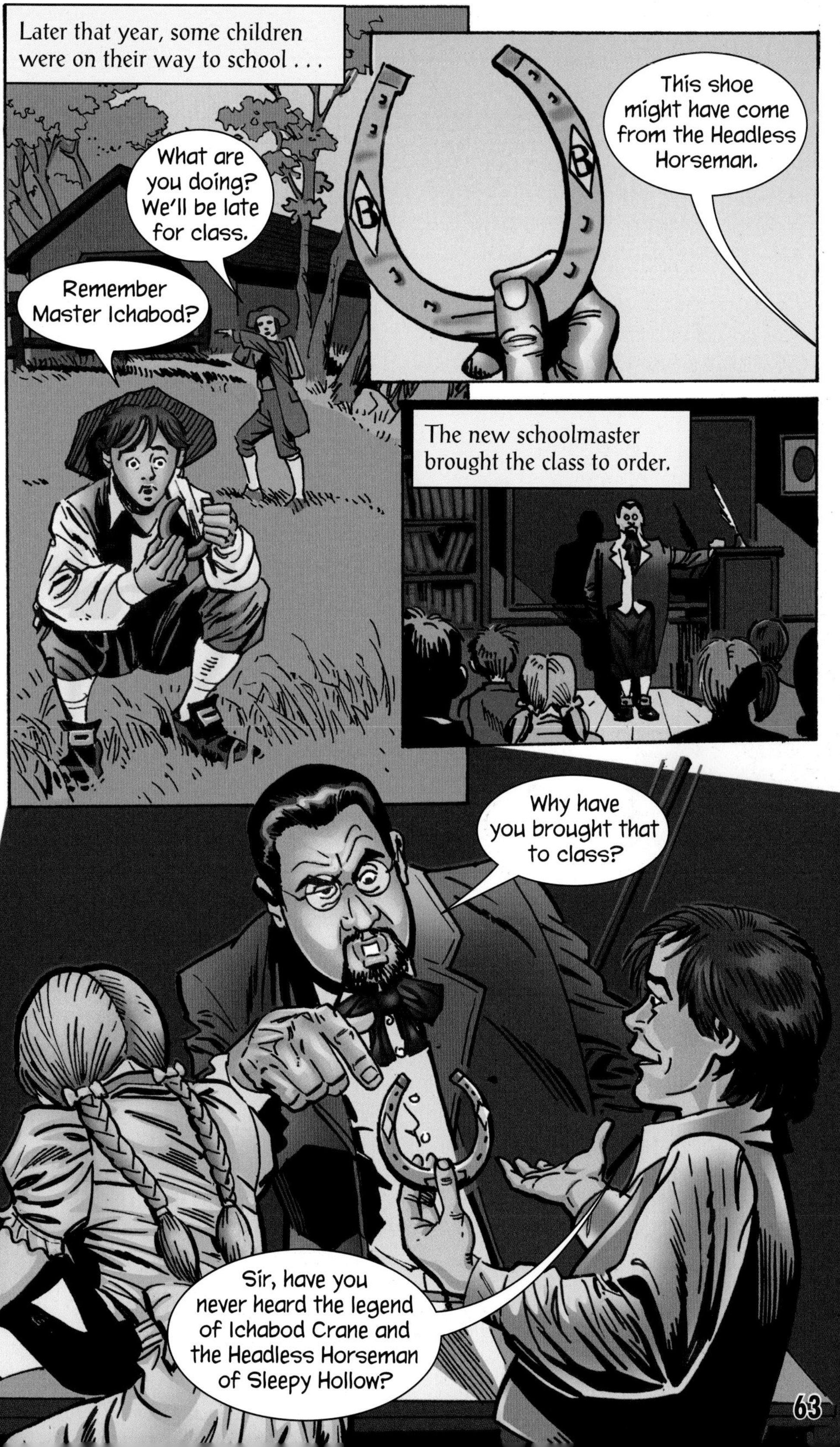
Later that year, some children were on their way to school . . .
What are you doing? We'll be late for class.
Remember Master Ichabod?
This shoe might have come from the Headless Horseman.
The new schoolmaster brought the class to order.
Why have you brought that to class?
Sir, have you never heard the legend of Ichabod Crane and the Headless Horseman of Sleepy Hollow?

About the Author

Washington Irving was born in New York City on April 3, 1789, toward the end of the Revolutionary War. His parents named him after George Washington. In 1809, Irving wrote his first book, *A History of New-York from the Beginning of the World to the End of the Dutch Dynasty*. This book poked fun at local history and politics. Irving wrote many other satires, humorous stories that commented on people's beliefs and politics. Two of his most famous short stories are "The Legend of Sleepy Hollow" and "Rip van Winkle." Irving became one of America's first authors to make a career as a writer, and he is considered the father of the American short story.

About the Retelling Author

Blake A. Hoena grew up in Wisconsin and then moved to Minnesota to go to school, receiving a Masters of Fine Arts degree in Creative Writing. Recently he's written a series of graphic novels about space alien brothers, Eek and Ack, who are forever trying to conquer Earth in zany ways.

About the Illustrator

Tod Smith grew up in Rhode Island, where he attended the Joe Kubert School of Cartoon and Graphic Art. He started working in comics in the 1980s, and has been an illustrator for comics and books ever since. He loves to play music in his free time, and when he was in middle school, the Beatles inspired him to start to play the guitar. He lives in Connecticut with his wife, Candace.

GLOSSARY

appetite (AP-uh-tite)—a desire or craving, often for food

bewitched (bi-WICHT)—to be haunted by a spell or curse

board (BORD)—to provide someone with food and a place to stay

crested (KRESS-tid)—reached the very top of something, such as a hill

gravity (GRAV-uh-tee)—the invisible force that pulls objects toward Earth's center

Hessian (HESH-uhn)—a German soldier hired by the British to fight the American colonists during the Revolutionary War (1775-1783)

steed (STEED)—a horse, especially a large, powerful one

superstition (soo-pur-STI-shuhn)—the belief in supernatural things, such as magic and ghosts

tarry (TAIR-ee)—to linger or wait around and do nothing

traitor (TRAY-tur)—someone who is disloyal to his or her country or government

THE STORY BEHIND
SLEEPY HOLLOW

Washington Irving is best known for writing "The Legend of Sleepy Hollow." He was also a biographer and historian. He liked to use real places, people, and events as the basis for his fictional stories.

Tarrytown lies along the eastern bank of the Hudson River, about 25 miles north of New York City. Irving actually spent the final years of his life living there. Today, there is also a small village called Sleepy Hollow just down the road from Tarrytown.

The church that Ichabod walks by on his way into Tarrytown is the Old Dutch Church of Sleepy Hollow. Built in 1685, it is one of the oldest churches in New York. Where the Headless Horseman was said to be buried is the Old Dutch Burying Grounds, next to the church. A nearby bridge crosses the Pocantico River.

Irving may have based his characters for "The Legend of Sleepy Hollow" on people he met and knew in the area. Many Van Tassels lived near Tarrytown. Eleanor Van Tassel Brush, the beautiful niece of Catriena Van Tassel, is said to have been Irving's model for Katrina. The local blacksmith, Abraham Martling, may have been the inspiration for Brom Bones. "Brom" was often a nickname for someone with the name Abraham.

The character of Ichabod Crane could have come from several sources. Irving probably borrowed the name from a soldier, Colonel Ichabod Crane, whom he met while serving in the army. Jesse Merwin, a schoolteacher from nearby Kinderhook, was a friend of Irving's and may have been the basis for Ichabod's character.

The capture of Major John André that was mentioned in "The Legend of Sleepy Hollow" was an important event during the Revolutionary War. On September 23, 1780, three local militiamen captured Major André in Tarrytown. He had made a plan with Benedict Arnold, and André's capture prevented an attack on the fort at West Point. Major André was convicted as a spy and later hanged.

There's also an actual legend about a Hessian soldier who was found in Sleepy Hollow. The Hessian was killed by soldiers of the Continental Army, and his head was nearly cut off. The legend says a local couple, out of respect for the Hessian, buried him in the Old Dutch Burying Grounds because a Hessian soldier had once saved their baby. Irving may have stumbled across this legend while working on a biography of George Washington, and it could have become the basis for "The Legend of Sleepy Hollow."

Discussion Questions

1. Toward the end of the story, some of the villagers from Tarry Town wonder what happened to Ichabod Crane. What do you think happened to him? Explain your answer using examples from the story to support your answer.

2. Ichabod Crane seems to enjoy listening to ghost stories, yet on pages 30 and 31, he explains why certain ghosts cannot exist. Why does Ichabod act this way? Why does he like ghost stories, yet is afraid of the ghosts in Sleepy Hollow?

3. Washington Irving actually wrote "The Legend of Sleepy Hollow" as a satire, a humorous story that commented on the lives of people living in upstate New York. Why do you think people now view it as a scary story?

WRITING PROMPTS

1. Do you have a favorite ghost story? Write it down.

2. At the end of the story, a new schoolmaster comes to Sleepy Hollow. Write a story about what happens to him. Does he encounter the Headless Horseman or another ghost?

3. Imagine that you lived in Tarry Town. Write a story about an encounter you would have with one of its many ghosts.

OTHER BOOKS

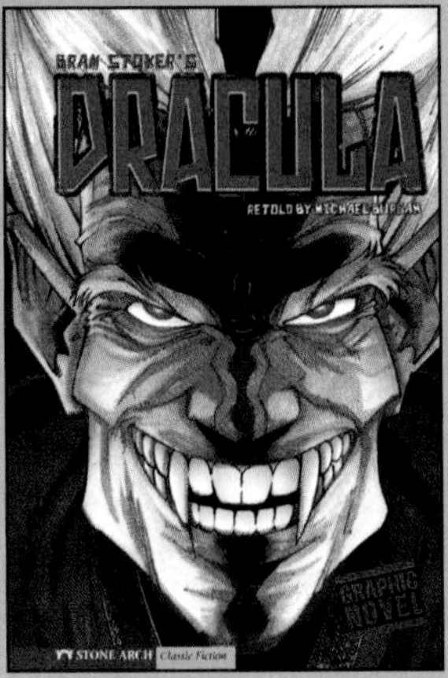
BRAM STOKER'S
DRACULA
RETOLD BY MICHAEL BURGAN
GRAPHIC NOVEL
STONE ARCH Classic Fiction

Dracula

On a business trip to Transylvania, Jonathan Harker stays at an eerie castle owned by a man named Count Dracula. When strange things start to happen, Harker investigates and finds the count sleeping in a coffin! Harker isn't safe, and when the count escapes to London, neither are his friends.

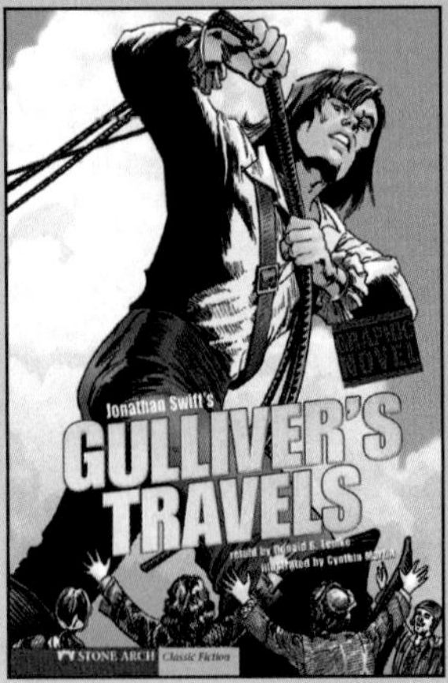
GRAPHIC NOVEL
Jonathan Swift's
GULLIVER'S TRAVELS
STONE ARCH Classic Fiction

Gulliver's Travels

Lemuel Gulliver always dreamed of sailing across seas, but he never could have imagined the places his travels would take him. On the island of Lilliput, he is captured by tiny creatures no more than six inches tall. In a country of Blefuscu, he is nearly squashed by an army of giants. His adventures could be the greatest tales ever told, if he survives long enough to tell them.

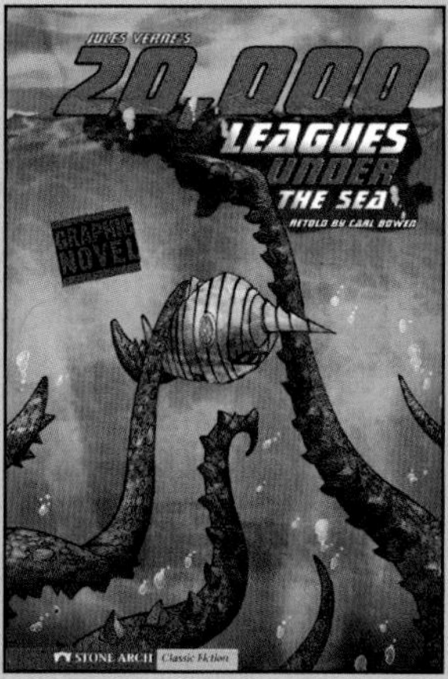
JULES VERNE'S
20,000
LEAGUES
UNDER
THE SEA
RETOLD BY CARL BOWEN
GRAPHIC NOVEL
STONE ARCH
Classic Fiction

20,000 Leagues Under the Sea

Scientist Pierre Aronnax and his trusty servant set sail to hunt a sea monster. With help from Ned Land, the world's greatest harpooner, the men soon discover that the creature is really a high-tech submarine. To keep this secret from being revealed, the sub's leader, Captain Nemo, takes the men hostage. Now, each man must decide whether to trust Nemo or try to escape this underwater world.

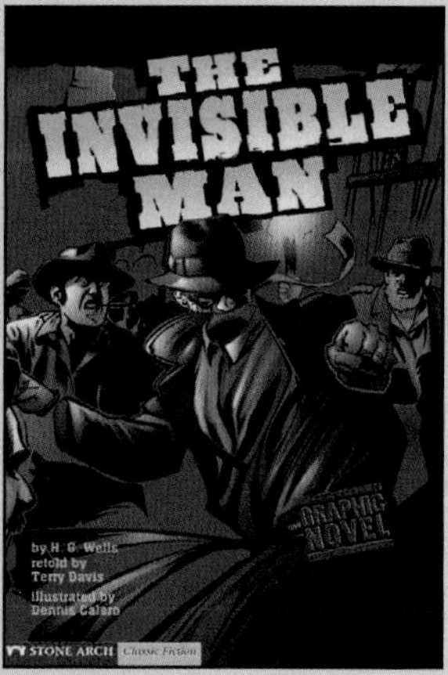
THE
INVISIBLE
MAN
GRAPHIC NOVEL
by H. G. Wells
retold by
Terry Davis
illustrated by
Dennis Calero
STONE ARCH
Classic Fiction

The Invisible Man

Late one night, a mysterious man wanders into a tiny English village. He is covered from head to toe in bandages. After a series of burglaries, the villagers grow suspicious. Who is this man? Where did he come from? When the villagers attempt to arrest the stranger, he suddenly reveals his secret —he is invisible! How can anyone stop the Invisible Man?

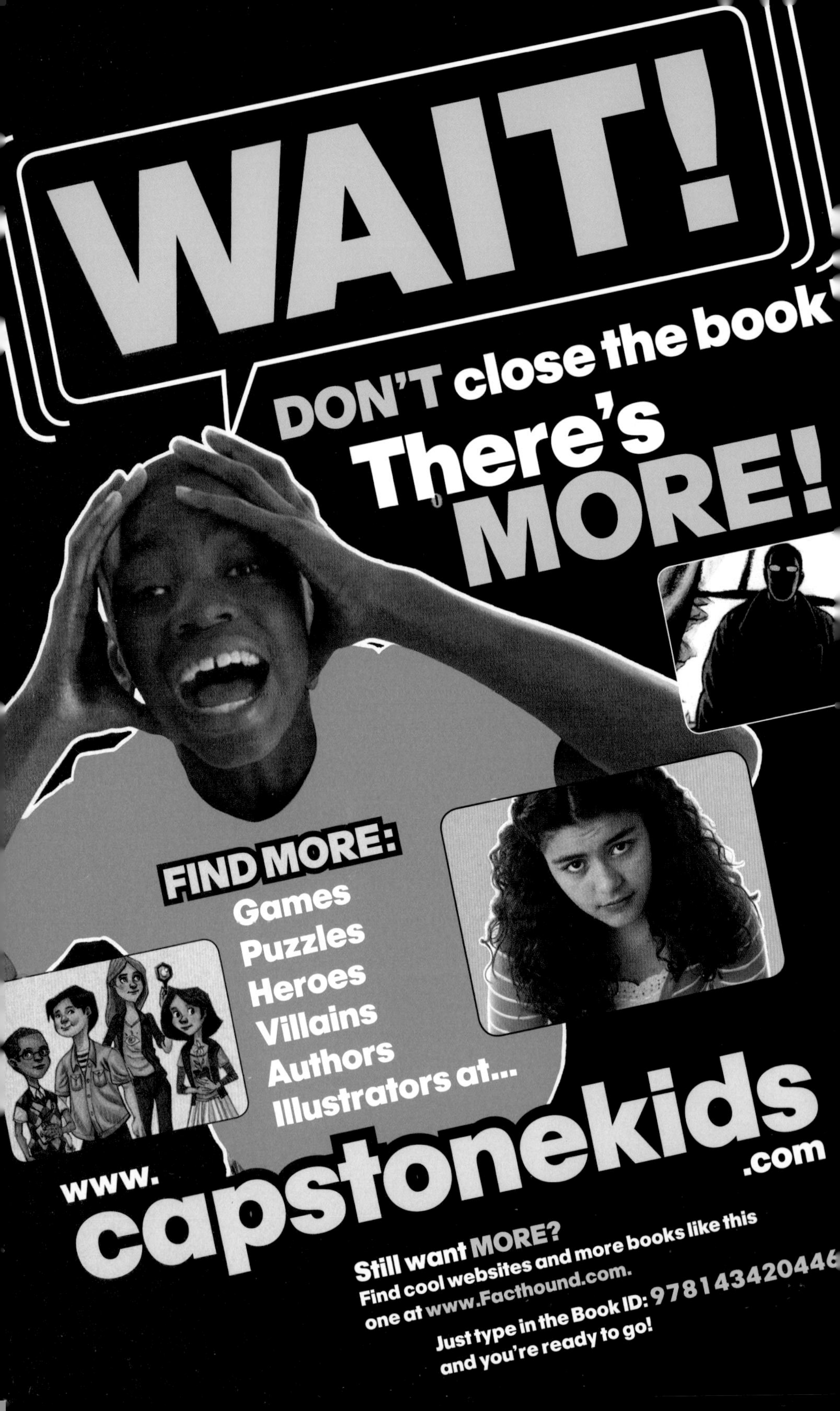
WAIT!
DON'T close the book!
There's MORE!
FIND MORE:
Games
Puzzles
Heroes
Villains
Authors
Illustrators at...
www.capstonekids.com
Still want MORE?
Find cool websites and more books like this one at www.Facthound.com.
Just type in the Book ID: 978143420446
and you're ready to go!